REBELLION

TYLER SVEC

Rebellion

This novel is a work of fiction. Names, descriptions,
entities, and incidents included in the story are products of
the author's imagination. Any resemblance to actual
persons, events and entities is entirely coincidental.

Cover Art courtesy of shutterstock.com
Cover Design by Tyler Svec
Interior Design by Tyler Svec

ISBN : 9798852407177

THE KINGDOM : II

REBELLION

TYLER SVEC

<u>Synopsis</u>

On his own for the first time, Roy Van Doren set off for his newly purchased cabin in the Appalachian Mountains. However, once he reached his cabin, he discovered that the upstairs room led him to another world.

After becoming lost in this new world, Roy met a family that became like his own and began to learn about this new life. They took Roy to the capital city, Sayatta, in order to register for the Hentar Academy, the leading school under the government known as the "Alliance".

Upon strong feelings against joining the Hentar Academy, Roy and his new friends, Alexander and Abigail, perchance met a man named Gideon who spoke of a different way, called the "Kingdom".

While the oldest brother, Cyrus, followed the path of a Hentar Knight, Roy and his friends attended the "Kingdom" and were soon being trained.

Many weeks passed as they were trained in armed, unarmed, and aerial combat. Cyrus became a Hentar Knight, and was presented the job of finding and helping to destroy the schools that did not partner with the Alliance.

When war finally broke out, Cyrus finally appeared to Roy and Alexander, asking for help to rescue three young girls from the city of Darsujes. Afterwards he parted with them.

As Roy and his friends closed in on the leader of the Alliance, Lucerine, it became clear that Roy was being targeted because he was an off-worlder. Under the guidance of their leader, Chrystar, Roy left and found his way back to the door he had first come through. As he left, he proposed to

Abigail and the two of them stepped through the doorway and entered into Roy's cabin in the Appalachian Mountains . . .

1

"**I DO BELIEVE,** this is my favorite place," Abby said. They sat on the front porch of their cabin, looking out towards the woods and low-laying lands beyond. The wind gently brushed through the trees, the leaves rustling as though they didn't have a care in the world.

"Definitely a good place to drink a cup of coffee with my wife," Roy said. He handed her a mug and sat down in the rocking chair next to her.

"You certainly have learned the way to my heart, Mr. Van Doren," Abby said. They both smiled.

"Likewise, Mrs.Van Doren." Roy said. "Now we just need to end this war, and we can get on with our lives."

"The war has already gone on for a year and a half, and I don't see it ending anytime soon."

"We'll have to wait and see," Roy said thoughtfully. "I have every confidence that Chrystar has a plan formed, and things will work out at just the right time."

"He is a good leader," Abby agreed. "I'm just growing weary of the war. I much prefer sitting on my porch drinking coffee to being caught in the middle of a great confrontation that I can't escape."

"True, very true," Roy said. "Nonetheless, I have no doubt we were put where we are for such a time as this. Even if we don't know why yet."

REBELLION

They were lost in their thoughts for a few minutes as Roy and Abby remembered how the war had started and how they had left and been forced to hide out in Roy's world for nearly six months. When it had been thought safe they had returned and now lived a life in both worlds, fighting in one and hiding in the other.

Their thoughts were interrupted as a low-flying blue Cessna airplane went right over the trees.

"The only thing disrupting this lovely day is that airplane," Abby noted.

"I'm starting to get a little intrigued about that airplane," Roy admitted. Abby shot him a quizzical look. "Three days in a row I've seen it flying all over these mountains, much lower than aircraft should be flying."

They watched as the plane circled in the distance and came closer to the cabin passing just over head. This time the plane was so low that Roy and Abby both flinched.

"Good grief! If he goes any lower, he'll be crashing into the trees!"

"Do you think we should be concerned?" Abby asked.

Roy thought for a moment. "I can't think of a serious reason to be concerned, but I should try to report him to authorities."

"You see? Griffin's are easier!"

"No argument there," Roy replied. "Much cheaper, too."

The plane made several more passes over the cabin, forcing them to retreat inside as they began to grow nervous. Finally, after a few more minutes the plane faded into the sky. They moved back out to the porch, once again enjoying the sunny day.

"At least in my world you don't have loud things like that to disrupt your day," Abby pointed out.

"Just imagine if I was to take you to a big city."

"I don't think that would be very enjoyable."

"Indeed. I much prefer our cabin in the woods. And I'm very glad that it has a secret door."

"What time are the others coming?" Abby asked. Immediately after she said the words, a loud crashing, tumbling, and yelling came from inside the cabin. They both jumped to their feet to see Jonathan standing amidst a sea of plates, bowls and silverware. He smiled sheepishly at them.

Roy turned to Abby. "Apparently, my dear, they are coming right now! Though they are much earlier than they are supposed to be."

"There's a perfectly good explanation, Captain," Jonathan said, standing straighter. "And don't worry. It goes beyond making a mess of your house." Roy took a step towards him, both of them determined to outlast the other. Finally, they both laughed.

"First things first, why did you bring all the dishes?" Abby asked.

"Tonight was the night, right?" Roy nodded.

"How many people are coming?"

"The A-Team," Jonathan answered hesitantly.

"All of them?"

"Well, a few people found out, then a few more found out . . .Yes, everyone's planning to be in attendance. Which is why I brought so many dishes. Now you don't have to spend all night cleaning up."

"For that, I thank you," Abby said. "Alexander and Savannah don't know about the reason for this get together, do they?"

"Nope. That has been kept strictly under wraps," Jonathan declared happily.

"Very good. Now, was there another reason you came ridiculously early?"

"Two, actually," Jonathan said, reaching into his pocket and pulling out a sealed envelope. "First, official orders!" Roy took the envelope and briefly studied it.

"Why are these opened?" Roy asked.

Jonathan looked at them in shock. "That *is* a most interesting question!"

"You, of course, realize I could have you court marshaled and sent to Sergeant Parks who would, most likely, yell at you for an hour an a half, as any drill sergeant is fond of doing. Furthermore, you do realize how utterly enjoyable I would find that?" Roy laughed, and soon everyone else joined in. "Good thing is, I trust you. But I take it your curiosity got the best of you?"

"Regrettably," Jonathan said. "Interesting stuff though."

"Just don't let it happen again!" Roy warned. They picked up the dishes and moved back out to the porch. Roy and Abby sunk into their rocking chairs while Jonathan sat on the railing. Roy pulled the papers out and quickly glanced over them. He turned to Abby. "It appears a small group from our team is being sent to Merodia."

"What's in Merodia?" Abby asked. "Seafaring city, is it not?"

"Yes, it is. I've been there once," Jonathan said. "A little freaky if you ask me. They make good money off of the underwater mining facilities."

"What do they mine?" Roy asked.

"Sactalines," Jonathan replied. "Almost a third of all the Alliance's sactalines come from Merodia."

"It's controlled by the Alliance?" Abby asked. Jonathan nodded. "Why are we being sent there?"

"There's a note with the orders," Jonathan said. Roy paged through and picked it out.

"It's from Chrystar," Roy said, reading aloud. "It says, 'Greetings to Roy and the A-Team. We have received coded letters from the city of Merodia in recent weeks, speaking of an informant that might hold valuable information that can be used in our fight against the Hentarian Knights and the Alliance. We have been communicating through coded letters and have agreed to unofficially send a small group, (no more than four) to try and

TYLER SVEC

make contact with the informant. At this moment the only name we can give you is *Trace*. I urge you to attempt to make contact with Trace and see what may come of it. Intelligence is not yet sure if this source can be completely trusted, so exercise extreme caution. In related events, we have captured a large number of Dreygars and they have grown quite fond of us. Gideon and Evelyn will make arrangements for you to use one of them on your mission. I wish you speed and safety and I look forward to hearing your report when you return!'

"Interesting," Abby said. Roy nodded. "Who gets the job?"

"The three of us and Wiggs will try to make contact, but we need to request three Dreygars because I want everyone else in the city within reasonable distance of our location. In case things go south."

"I'm sure Chrystar will agree with that," Jonathan replied.

"Make the preparations after supper," Roy ordered. Jonathan smiled but didn't move, instead choosing to keep smiling stupidly at Roy for several seconds. "I seem to remember now, that you said there were two reasons that you came early...and I'm now thinking you must want to do something else?"

"Yes, Captain," Jonathan said. "Alexander's coming, he just doesn't know why, per-se. He put in a formal request that you acquire some Cabin Juice."

"Cabin Juice?" Abby asked. Roy also gave a confused look.

"That's what he called it. He said you smuggled it to his wedding as the refreshment of choice. It was green and and had bubbles in it. Little bottle about yea big." Jonathan motioned with his hands to an approximate size.

"Ah, yes!" Roy said, remembering. "I believe Alexander is referencing a drink called Mountain Dew."

"That's it!" Jonathan exclaimed. "Mountain Dew! Can we get some?"

"I don't think we have time to get it before supper, but I promise before

5

we leave in the morning, I'll get some for all of us."

"Can I come?" Jonathan asked with a childish grin on his face. "You've never taken me into town before."

"Sure you can come. Do you really think *smuggled* is the right word to use?" Roy asked. "It's certainly not that hard to acquire it and take it through the upstairs door."

"No, but you must put yourself in our shoes. We *know* a guy. Who can get *stuff* that no one else can get!"

"It does sound kind of awesome," Abby said. Roy nodded his agreement.

Their attention was pulled to the sky again as the dark blue Cessna airplane once again appeared and began circling.

"Two times in one day," Abby noted. Roy nodded. Jonathan looked at it, dumbfounded.

"What is that thing?" Jonathan asked. They watched as it went below the treeline, likely landing in the open field below.

"It's called an airplane," Roy explained. "It's how we fly in our world. How about we all take a stroll to see what's going on?"

Ten minutes later they walked into the large field Roy thought the airplane would be in. They scanned the horizon finally spotting the dark blue Cessna sitting three hundred feet to their left.

Roy spotted the pilot, sitting on the ground in front of the plane, resting his back against the tire. A cheeseburger and milkshake were in either hand.

If he had been standing he would have been mid height. He was clad in a brown leather coat and had a bushy mustache and eyebrows that were equally bushy. It was evident they had been spotted as the man raised his milkshake up as if trying to wave and say hello, despite his mouth being full of cheeseburger.

"Of all the things I expected to find down here, you were not one of them!" Roy called out.

"Hey! Hey! My long lost brother!" the man climbed to his feet and began coming towards them.

"Brother?" Abby asked. Roy didn't get a chance to reply as his brother embraced him.

"You weren't kidding when you said this place was hard to find! I had to buzz the mountainside for nearly a week to find it!"

"I'm surprised you did," Roy managed as he tried to get his bearings. "I'm surprised to see you...here."

"Be glad you are, because you almost didn't. That airfield in Granville has been closed for almost two days."

"That's unusual," Abby whispered. Roy nodded his agreement.

"And who are these people?" Geoffrey asked.

"Introductions are in order," Roy said. "Everyone, I'd like you to meet my brother Geoffrey."

"You two are brothers?" Jonathan asked. Roy and Geoffrey nodded their heads. "You look nothing alike."

"Bet you haven't heard that one before have you, Roy?" Geoffrey teased.

"Only every day of our lives growing up."

"Roy and I were the weird ones in the family, because we didn't look like mom or dad...maybe we were adopted."

"Or we just got all those genetics that our parents lacked?"

"That works. So who are these people?"

"Sorry, Geoffrey. This is my wife, Abigail, and our good friend, Jonathan."

"Holy cheeseburgers! Did you say 'wife'?"

"Yes I did," Roy said, unable to hide his smile any longer. Geoffrey laughed.

"Now I know why you haven't come to visit me. Let me guess, she came with the cabin?"

Roy thought for a moment.

"Kind of," Abby interjected. In an instant Geoffrey embraced her.

"It's nice to meet you, *sister-in-law!* I'm sorry for you that you have to have a brother-in-law like me."

"Just don't make a mess of my house and we'll be just fine."

Geoffrey looked at Roy with a smile. "I like her." He turned to Abby. "You don't happen to have a sister do you?"

"Sorry, I was not blessed with sisters."

He looked at Roy. "Well, you win some, and loose some."

"Looks like you won a plane. How did you manage that?" Roy asked.

Geoffrey's face beamed as he turned to look at the plane. "Roy and Abby Van Doren, and friend Jonathan. I would like you to meet the newest member of my family. I call her the *Berry-High-Flyer.*"

"That is a very unusual name," Abby noted.

Geoffrey just shrugged. "When Aunt Charlotte died, her Will stipulated that she had a large chunk of money set aside for certain extended family members that she liked, and I was one of them. So I bought the *Berry-High-Flyer* and have taken a job as a mail carrier."

"So you fly the mail in?" Roy asked.

"Yes, sirree! Once I figured out I was close to your place, I took it upon myself to try and find it. Yours was the only cabin to be found."

"Well, I suppose it should only suffice to invite you to dinner," Abby said.

Geoffrey beamed. "Home cooking is always far better than fast food," he exclaimed. "How close are we to the cabin?"

"About ten minutes walk," Roy answered. They started walking down the open field to the path before having to stop and look behind them to see Jonathan studying and cautiously touching the airplane.

8

"It's a beauty, isn't she?" Geoffrey asked.

"How does it work?" Jonathan asked, clearly enthralled. Geoffrey walked back to him, giving him a tour of the plane, all the while Jonathan stared at the plane in awe and wonder.

"Do you think it was wise to invite him to supper?" Roy asked.

"He's your brother and he went to great effort to find you!" Abby exclaimed. "What else was I suppose to do? You had said you and your brother got along now."

"We do, we do. That's not in question," Roy replied, thinking. "But what are we going to say when the entire A-Team starts coming through the upstairs door?"

"Hadn't thought of that." They both fell silent for a minute.

"I'll do my best to keep him outside, and just follow my lead on everything else," Roy finally said. Abby hastily nodded agreement as Geoffrey came walking towards them once again.

"Roy! I'm not sure about your friend there. He *claims* to have never seen an airplane before."

"He doesn't get out much," Roy replied.

"I'll say," Geoffrey agreed. He and Abby continued up the path, and Jonathan soon joined Roy.

"I officially do not understand your world, but there are certainly some things that are mind-blowing," Jonathan said, trying to keep his voice to a whisper.

"Now you understand how I felt when I first discovered the door in the upstairs."

"I suppose," Jonathan agreed. They followed Geoffrey and Abby up the hill, both of them wondering just what would happen when they reached the cabin. Abby exchanged a halfway nervous glance, but otherwise held her composure and masterfully dealt with the seemingly overexcited

Geoffrey.

They reached the small clearing the cabin sat in. Immediately, Geoffrey nodded his head in approval.

"Good job on the house!" Geoffrey congratulated. "I remember seeing the first pictures you had of this place. I was seriously wondering about your intelligence in making such a purchase."

"Roy's fixed up the place real nice, hasn't he?" Abby asked.

Geoffrey nodded. "I think I'll hire you to come remodel my house," he said.

"Can I get you boys anything to drink?" Abby asked.

"I'll take some good ole water from the tap," Geoffrey said, sinking into the rocking chair.

"You sure? We have some ice tea," Abby offered.

"No thanks. Never been a fan of tea. Besides I need something to wash down this milkshake with."

"Jonathan?"

"I'll hold out for Cabin Juice."

"What's Cabin Juice?" Geoffrey asked.

"Never mind," Roy interjected. Abby disappeared inside and came out a moment later with three cups of water. Geoffrey offered his thanks and drank it in one gulp.

They talked for several minutes as though they were old friends. Roy smiled to himself, not able to remember the last time he and his brother had had a conversation that felt this good. Though once they had been far from each other, over the past few months they had begun to rebuild their relationship.

Abby and Jonathan carried on with Geoffrey, too, as though he was an old friend, and before long no one even bothered to keep track of the time. The smell of good cooking wafted from the kitchen and out to the front

10

porch; filling the entire clearing.

Suddenly voices filled the inside of the cabin and panic flooded into Roy. Jonathan shared his concern, already knowing what had happened. Geoffrey, who was just as surprised by the voices as they were, stood and looked inside at ten members of the A-Team who had just passed through the upstairs door, with the intention of joining them for supper.

"Woah, we're having a party aren't we? Who are these people?"

"Friends of ours...from church," Roy fibbed.

"Nice. I have to meet them!"

Before Roy and Jonathan could distract him in any way Geoffrey had already made his way into the crowd and was happily chatting up a storm with everyone he met. Abby gave an amused look and quickly came over to them.

"I'm both annoyed, frustrated and amused by this scenario," Abby admitted. "I'm not sure which reaction I should listen to."

"Let's go with *amused*."

"It is rather funny watching everyone else talk to him, when they clearly have no idea who he is," Jonathan pointed out. They watched for several minutes, noticing the blank and confused expressions that were on everyone's faces after they were done talking to Geoffrey. Eventually Geoffrey returned to them.

"You got some nice friends here, Roy. I'd say you've done quite well for yourself."

"Thank you," Roy replied. The upstairs door opened and Abby's parents, Norah and Victor came walking down the stairs.

"More people?" Geoffrey asked. "Where are all these people coming from?" They all stammered, trying to come up with an explanation. A few seconds later the door opened again a eight more members and Evelyn came down the stairs. "Good grief, what do you have up there, a hotel?"

"It's nothing really, just an old attic with mice and mothballs," Roy managed.

"Roy Van Doren, you never could bluff worth beans. You're hiding something up there."

"I can assure you there's nothing there."

"I'm going to see if for myself."

"Oh, no!" Roy and Abby exclaimed as Geoffrey sprinted up the stairs and into the upstairs room. They reached the room to see a confused Geoffrey studying everything. At the far end of the room, the door appeared in the wall as it always was.

"Okay, so you weren't bluffing," Geoffrey finally said. "But there's still something strange about this room."

"Strange?" Abby asked, casually stepping between him and the door.

"Yeah, I'm sure most of the people have come through this room, because there are no cars outside."

"How's that possible?" Jonathan asked.

Geoffrey contemplated the question for the moment. "I have no idea," he finally admitted. "But I think the answer lies behind that door."

"I think the food's almost done!" Abby said. "Let's eat supper and then contemplate this?"

"Sounds fair," Geoffrey agreed. They turned and began walking towards the stairwell, each breathing a sigh of relief. In an instant their relief turned to panic as Geoffrey laughed childishly and sprinted towards the door in the wall. In an instant he threw open the door, rushed through. Roy and the others cried out as the door disappeared and Geoffrey vanished into the other world.

2

GEOFFREY'S JOY TURNED into panic as the cabin somehow vanished and he found himself instead tumbling and tripping through a deep leafy forest of underbrush. He cried out as a person appeared in front of him and then was barreled to the ground as they both rolled down the hill until they came to a sudden stop at the bottom.

"Holy cheeseburgers! What just happened?" Geoffrey asked, mostly talking to himself. Geoffrey sat up, finding that he was in the middle of a dense forest. It appeared to be the middle of the night, and everything was covered in shadows.

"Off-worlders and their ridiculous expressions!" a voice exclaimed. "Who ever heard of something called a cheeseburger? I'm almost afraid to ask what a *cheeseburger* is!" The man floundered to his feet and looked right at him. "Just so you know, there are two sides of a door. Have you never heard of *walking* through it? "

"Sorry," was all Geoffrey was able to mutter. The man straightened in the dark. He cautiously stepped forward.

"You're not Roy?" the man said. Geoffrey was dumbfounded, still struggling to find any words.

"No. I'm not Roy."

"I can hear that. Who are you?"

"Where am I?"

"My question first," the man argued.

Geoffrey shrugged. "I'm Geoffrey."

"Geoffrey...Geoffrey?" the man asked, as though in great thought. "I've heard that name before. Where?"

"Roy had a brother named Geoffrey I think," a woman's voice said behind him. Geoffrey jumped back against a tree. The two people came towards him. Now he could see they were wearing a strange kind of armor, with swords to their sides and crossbows in their hands. One had a glowing green light in the middle of their chest.

"How did you come to be here?" the man asked. "And have you heard the name Roy Van Doren before?"

"Yes," Geoffrey stammered. "I-"

"How do you know him?" the woman asked.

"He's my brother," Geoffrey answered. Neither of them moved. "Would someone please tell me where I am and what's going on!"

"You're here without Roy?" the woman asked. Geoffrey nodded. Still their faces were clouded in shadows. The two figures looked at each other.

"This is interesting," the man said. The two figures seemed to relax, but Geoffrey still felt nervous.

"It is a pleasure to meet you," the woman said. She reached to a bag slung over her shoulder and pulled out another large glowing stone. It was neon orange. She whistled and the stone flew into the tree above them. Within a second they were surrounded by daylight. Geoffrey struggled to keep conscious as he wondered what was going on. Was it actually night, or was it now day? He closed his eyes tight, wondering if he would open them and still see the same thing.

"Who-who-who are you?"

"Friends of Roy," the man said. "My name is Alexander, and this is my wife Savannah." Geoffrey looked at them skeptically.

"Pleasure to meet you," Savannah greeted. Geoffrey could now see both their faces and wasn't nearly as frightened by them as he had been at first, still his mind struggled to make sense of what was going on.

"What is going on?" Geoffrey asked.

Alexander started laughing. "I have seen that face before! That face of absolute befuddlement! Now I can see a resemblance between you and Roy."

"What is going on?" Geoffrey asked again, wishing this nightmare would be over soon.

"Don't worry. It's easy to explain," Savannah reassured. "Come with us." Together the three of them walked up the hillside they had just tumbled down. Geoffrey looked at the source of the light again, marveling at the strange stone.

"I'm confused," Geoffrey said as they climbed. "Is it day or is it night?"

"Both."

"How can it possibly be both?"

"It is day time. But this area is heavily controlled by the Alliance. The Alliance has destroyed so much that is good. As a result of the wickedness, the sun seldom shines here anymore." Geoffrey refrained from asking anymore questions and instead just followed. Finally they reached the place where Geoffrey and Alexander had fallen from.

Alexander and Savannah stood there, as though they expected something to happen. Geoffrey watched with great interest as nothing happened for almost a minute.

"This is unusual," Alexander said.

"Why can't we get through?" Savannah asked.

"Get through what?" Geoffrey asked.

"The door that you came through in the upstairs of Roy's cabin. It leads right here!"

"Where's the door?"

"That's kind of the problem. The door isn't here, even though it's here-or it suppose to be here-but it's not here at the moment," Alexander explained. He turned back to the forest in front of them. "Hello! Door! Show yourself!" Several moments passed without anything happening. "HEY! OPEN THE DOOR!"

"Hon, I think the door is gone," Savannah said.

"Where did it go?" Geoffrey asked.

"This is what I'm trying to figure out!" Alexander exclaimed. Geoffrey couldn't help but chuckle.

"It looks more like your yelling at trees," Savannah pointed out. Alexander gave her an exasperated expression and then turned back to where the door should've been.

"Hello!" Alexander said. "Where are you, magic door?!"

"Hey guys, I can hear him!" came a voice. The voice was muffled but otherwise clear. Geoffrey recognized it as Jonathan. There was a great chorus of voices until finally they were quieted, a moment later. *"Alexander, can you hear me?"*

Alexander looked nearly as stunned as Geoffrey felt. "Yes."

"Can you hear us?" Jonathan asked again.

"I can hear you! Can you hear me?"

"Yes, we can hear you."

"What happened?" Alexander asked. There was once again a great commotion of voices until Roy's broke through the rest.

"Is Geoffrey there?"

"Yes. We ran into each other." Alexander gave Geoffrey an amused look. "What exactly happened?"

"Hey, Geoffrey?" Roy's voice called out.

"Yes," Geoffrey called out cautiously.

"So, big news, this cabin is a bit special. That door we told you not to go through comes out to the forest you're in now."

"So where am I?" Geoffrey asked. "Am I in Vermont still?"

"Yes, but no." Roy started. *"It's weird, but I think you're still in the cabin, somehow. Or else the cabin is in the other world-the world you're now stuck in. I've heard from a few other off-worlders that once new people go through the door, the door will disappear for a while."*

"I'm in another world?" Geoffrey asked, his mind and head swimming in all the sci-fi novels he had read as a kid. "How is that possible?"

"I'm not really sure, but it is. I discovered it by accident the first day I moved up here and didn't come back for some time. It's where I met Abigail."

"So Abigail literally came with the cabin?" Geoffrey teased.

"Yep." A moment of silence passed between all of them.

"So what now?" Savannah asked. "There must be a way for the door to reappear?"

"Chrystar said it stays closed until the person who passed through it is ready to go back," Roy explained. *"I think you're stuck."*

"Comforting," Geoffrey muttered.

"Maybe if we knock him out the door will reappear and at least Savannah and I can come through," Alexander suggested. Savannah gave him a look.

"We can't just leave him here, unconscious," Savannah replied.

"Of course not, my dear! We knock him out, the door appears, and we drag him through!"

"If he can't go through it when he's awake, why would he be able to go through it when he's asleep?"

"Because he doesn't know he's going through the door?" Alexander suggested. "It's all in his mind?"

"That doesn't make any sense. If you follow that logic, we're all in his mind and aren't real."

"That's not what I meant!"

"It's what you implied," Jonathan retorted from the other side.

"So we knock him unconscious?" Alexander asked again.

Geoffrey shook his head, hoping this was all a bad dream. "For what it's worth, the guy who would be unconscious for all of this, is not interested."

"Take one for the team," Alexander said. Savannah rolled her eyes.

"You're not knocking out my brother!" Roy yelled from the other side.

"Okay, fine, what other ideas are there to make the door appear?"

What happened next was almost too much for Geoffrey to comprehend as a commotion greater than any he had heard, echoed from the other side. Everything was indistinct and muffled. A second later a blinding light flashed in front of them. The force of the explosion threw them all from their feet. The three of them laid on the ground, too stunned to get up. When finally they did, they could see that smoke was rising from where they had been standing. The vegetation in a five foot circle was blackened and burnt.

They climbed back to the spot, hesitant to speak.

"Are you okay?" Jonathan's voice came.

"By some miracle we're alive," Geoffrey answered. "What just happened?" A great commotion of voices came through until Roy silenced them.

"Abigail had an interesting idea of trying to use some Tantine arrows to blow a hole through to the other world."

"Seems like a logical idea," Savannah said.

"Yes, well, now we have a very sizable whole in the upstairs wall!"

"Great! That means you can step through the door right?"

"Not exactly. I'm looking at a forest, but it's not the one you three are

18

in," Roy answered. *"I'm looking directly into my backyard."*

"Oh...I see." Alexander pondered for a moment. "Maybe you can step out the hole and actually end up here instead?"

A moment of silence passed.

"That's a negatory," Roy answered. *"We just dropped a rock out the hole and it hit the ground."*

"So how do we get out of this predicament?" Geoffrey asked.

"Let's focus on what we know," Roy's voice came again. *"Geoffrey, for whatever reason, you're stuck in that world and that means you've officially joined the A-Team. Alexander, we have an assignment we were going to start in the morning. It's your job now."* Roy quickly read the orders to them. *"Before you do any of this though, you need to contact Gideon and Chrystar and get them to come here, or make contact in some way. If anyone can solve this mystery, it'll be the two of them. We'll remain where we are until we hear from them."*

"Roy, I know this is probably obvious, but I still have no idea what's going on," Geoffrey said.

"I know," came the reply. *"But I also know you can roll with the punches and will do fine. Try your best to learn everything Savannah and Alexander teach you, and good luck."*

"You have more faith than I do," Geoffrey acknowledged. Silence passed.

"Maybe that's why you're here." Roy said, and Geoffrey was lost in his thoughts for a moment. *"Happy Anniversary Savannah and Alexander. We were going to have a surprise party for you."*

"It was certainly a surprise!" Alexander beamed, winking at Savannah.

"Good luck and we hope to hear from you soon!"

Savannah held her hand out and the glowing rock that she had released into the air came back to her hand. The light vanished leaving them once

19

again in darkness.

"Greeting's Geoffrey, I would like to officially welcome you to the A-Team!" Alexander said, shaking his hand.

"The A-Team? He calls it the A-Team?"

"I still think it's a weird name." They motioned for him to follow and they began walking through the darkened forest.

"What is the glowing light?" Geoffrey asked.

"It's called a Sactaline," Savannah answered. "They are a small phosphorescent stone, each color has a different attribute. I'm a pilot, so I was given a green one. Roy said it works something like a radio."

"A radio?" Geoffrey asked, peace coming over him. "Finally something I know...and you said you're a pilot? That's great! Where's your plane?"

"What's a plane?" Alexander asked.

Geoffrey's mind spun in circles. "Never mind."

"Around here we don't fly planes. We fly Griffins," Savannah explained.

"*Griffins?*"

"Don't worry you'll get used to all of this," Savannah reassured.

"I'm not so sure about that." Savannah reached into a bag and pulled out a few small Sactalines that were black on the outside. "Touch these."

Geoffrey hesitantly obeyed, his breath taken away as he discovered that almost instantly he was adorned in the same armor or uniform that they were wearing. Geoffrey marveled at the armor as they came to a stop in a large clearing.

"What are we waiting for?" Geoffrey asked.

"Dawnchaser," Savannah answered. A moment later Dawnchaser landed in the clearing in front of them. Geoffrey felt his mouth drop open as he looked into the eyes of the massive Griffin. He could faintly see Alexander and Savannah both smiling at him, as though they were parents waiting for kids to open their gifts. Geoffrey was speechless as he looked into the eyes of the Griffin.

In an instant Geoffrey felt his head swimming, his brain having had too much to process in a such a short amount of time. Geoffrey shook his head, and then fainted on the forest floor.

3

"THIS REALLY DOES make it feel much more open," Abby commented. She and Roy were the only ones still in the upstairs room of the cabin, looking out through the giant hole in the wall. "Never know what's going to happen in your day."

"Brother visits, friends visit, brother gets stuck in other world, door disappears, hole gets blown in the side of the house. Yep. It's been a full day," Roy replied.

"Sorry about the house."

"It's okay. I'll just go to town and get some wood. Not like we have anything else to do right now?" They both chuckled. "We'll have it patched up by nightfall. I think I'll take Jonathan with me."

"You will have a very happy Jonathan," Abby said. "If you're going to town, I will make you a grocery list, too. Feeding this many people for so long was not in the plan."

They walked downstairs where everyone was gathered either in the living room or on the front porch. Roy and Abby went to the living room, with everyone joining them. With so many people, the cabin definitely looked smaller than usual.

"Welcome to our house," Roy said. "I know for most of you this is your first time." Several nodded and shook their heads in approval. "I hope you like it because I don't think we can get back home; not for a while anyway."

"Do we have any kind of a plan?" Evelyn asked.

"First and foremost, Jonathan and I are going into town to get some wood to fix the house."

"Town?" Jonathan asked. "You're taking me with you?"

"Yes, and sorry. Right now I'm only going to take Jonathan." A disappointed moan went through the group. Roy smiled to himself, feeling like a parent choosing which kid was going to come with him.

"Hopefully Gideon and Chrystar can get back to us soon so we can start unraveling this mystery." Roy turned to Evelyn. "Were Gideon and the girls supposed to be coming?"

Everyone remembered how they had helped Cyrus rescue the three young girls, Ember, Henley, and Bristol from the city of Darsujes, at the beginning of the war.

The girls and Cyrus's motives were one of the biggest mysteries that had yet to be solved. They had given their names and ages willingly, but beyond that no other evidence of them could be found. They had searched though countless databases and files for any records of children or citizens with the last name Apelman. But none had ever been found.

Gideon and Evelyn, having never been able to have children, had happily stepped up to adopt the three girls.

"No. We weren't quite ready to bring them here. Besides, Gideon said he had a mountain of paperwork to finish. It shouldn't take long for Alexander and Savannah to get word to him."

"Good. In that case I want someone in the upstairs waiting to hear back. The rest of you, let's put your outdoors and hunting skills to work and go catch us some food for tomorrow's supper." The group dispersed with large numbers of them heading outside.

"Do us all a favor and don't get lost!" Roy called out after them.

"I wouldn't worry about them too much, my dear, they are some of the best trackers in the business," Abby reminded.

"True, but they haven't been in this world before. At least most of them." Roy replied. "I hope Geoffrey does okay. I know from experience, the first day is the hardest."

"I may not have met Geoffrey for very long, but I think he's going to get more than he bargained for; having to be with Alexander all day," Evelyn stated.

"I'm sure everyone will have quite a tale to tell when they come back," Abby replied.

"You ready, Jonathan?"

"Yes, sir!" Jonathan jumped from his spot with a childish grin on his face. "Hey, Roy? Do you suppose when we're in this town of yours, we would be able to get some Cabin Juice?"

"Of course we can get some Cabin Juice," Roy answered. Roy quickly got his wallet and keys and went out to where the truck was waiting for them. Roy stifled a laugh as he saw everyone carefully studying it, and inspecting the rubber tires with great curiosity.

"Is this thing safe?" Jonathan asked. "And how on earth does this work?"

"Get in and I'll show you." They both climbed in. Roy put his seat-belt on and Jonathan carefully watched and then copied him. Roy turned the key and the engine came to life.

"This is a little freaky," Jonathan said, as Roy began to turn the truck around. Roy made his way to the road and headed to the left as they wound through the mountains. A few minutes later Jonathan was clearly enjoying himself.

"This is cool!" Jonathan exclaimed. He began looking to the dashboard. "What's this?" He pointed to a large black button.

"Power button for the radio...don't touch it!"

"Why not?" Jonathan asked, his finger hovering in front of the button.

"Just don't. Next time you see Alexander ask him about his experience."

Twenty minutes later they rolled into a small town.

"Welcome to Granville, Vermont!" Roy declared as they entered into the small but cozy town.

"You weren't kidding about small were you?" Jonathan asked, looking at everything like a kid would look at Christmas presents.

"Population, 349. It's only varied by ten or twenty in the past thirty years, or so I'm told." They continued driving down the main street, where a number of houses were tucked away in the trees.

"This is cool. Your world has much different towns than we do."

"Just imagine if I was to take you into a city," Roy replied with a chuckle.

"Seems like a very peaceful place to live," Jonathan concluded. "But so far I've hardly seen any people."

"The town may not look like much, but it has a church, a diner, a small school, a bank, various stores and other shops and at the end of it all is *Hendrix Groceries*."

"Is that where we get Cabin Juice?"

"Yes, that's where we get the Mountain Dew." Roy parked the truck in the small rundown parking lot which was next to a building that looked as though it hadn't been painted for twenty years.

"This place looks old," Jonathan said.

"It's been here for nearly eighty years, third generation family business. Just changed hands." They got out of the truck and Jonathan looked around skeptically.

"What's wrong?"

"I seriously haven't seen a single person in this town yet," Jonathan noted.

"I wouldn't worry to much, this time of night, a large portion of the town ends up at Terra's, a few miles south."

"Terra's?"

"Local bar. Great burgers, but that's about all I'm interested in." They slowly walked towards the door. Roy stopped short of the door, motioning for Jonathan to come close.

"Keep your head up and try to act like you live in this world. Everyone in the town thinks that Abby and I are spies or something of the sort."

"Spies?"

"It was the easiest way to explain why we vanish for long periods of time," Roy said. "I let them believe it, because they would think I was crazy if I told them the truth."

"Fair enough," Jonathan agreed. "Don't worry. I can act totally normal."

"I believe it. Just be glad you didn't see Alexander the one and only time I took him into town."

"I heard stories of that. Legendary."

"Follow my lead." Roy rounded the corner and pulled the door open, walking into the small grocery store that had everything you might ever need in the smallest space you could ever imagine.

"This is awesome!" Jonathan exclaimed happily as he surveyed the countless shelves and displays. "Where's the Cabin Juice?"

"Right here," Roy answered pointing to a refrigerated cooler on the left. Jonathan looked at it, his mouth gaping open.

"So many!" Jonathan exclaimed. "Why are they different colors?"

"Different kinds," Roy answered. "The one we usually get is called Mountain Dew."

"That's still a weird name for it, because I'm pretty sure it does not taste like dew."

"Very true, but for what it's worth you can choose Dr. Pepper, Root Beer,

Ginger Ale-"

"Dr. Pepper?" Jonathan asked, wrinkling up his brow. "It's medicine?"

"No, it's just the name."

"Why would you name it *Dr.* Pepper if it's not medicine? Was it made by a doctor?"

"If my memory serves me correctly, it was created by a pharmacist named Charles Alderton."

"So not a doctor?"

"Well...he was a pharmacist."

"He was a farmer?"

"No. He was-ah, never mind."

"Okay. If it's all the same to you, I'll stick with Cabin Juice."

"Mountain Dew it is! Go ahead and get one."

Jonathan gleefully grabbed a bottle from the cooler as they made their way up to the front desk. They stood waiting for a minute before Roy finally called out.

A young blond haired girl came from the back room. She smiled warmly as she walked in.

"Good afternoon, Mr. Van Doren," she greeted.

He smiled and tipped his hat. "Good afternoon, Miss Hendrix."

"Got a shopping list for me?"

"Sure do." Roy answered handing the list to the woman.

"Who's your friend?"

"Sylvia Hendrix, I would like you to meet Jonathan Analai. Jonathan, Sylvia. He's a good friend of mind who's visiting for...well, it might be quite a while."

"Always nice to see a new face around here," Sylvia replied, shaking Jonathan's hand. "I'll take care of this list for you and be right back."

Before they knew what was happening Sylvia was scurrying all over the store, grabbing items on the shelf, faster than Roy or Jonathan would have been able to find them. Finally, she set the last item on the counter.

She looked at Jonathan, intently for a moment. "Are you a spy, too?"

"Depends on who's asking," Jonathan replied. "To some I say, *'I could tell you but then I'd have to kill you'*, but to people I like, I reply *'Only on weekdays'*."

"Which list am I on?"

"The second one, of course."

"Then I am honored to be on the list of people you like," Sylvia teased.

"You have Cabin Juice! How could I not?"

"What?"

"Mountain Dew!" Roy interjected.

"Yes, exactly. Mountain Dew," Jonathan affirmed.

"I can see the way to your heart is through Mountain Dew," Sylvia said.

"You know it!" Jonathan exclaimed. "Do you have any more?"

"I just got a full case of it this morning."

"We'll take it!" Jonathan said.

"The whole thing?" Sylvia asked, seeming surprised and amused. Roy hesitated.

"Yes, the whole thing," Roy stammered. "Big get-together this weekend, and Mountain Dew seems to be the drink of choice."

"To each their own. At least you're not spending your time and money down at Terra's," Sylvia replied. Roy nodded his approval. "Are we going to see you and Abby at church this week?"

"Maybe, but we're kind of in the middle of a...project," Roy answered.

"That's too bad."

"You can thank him," Roy said, jabbing Jonathan in the side. Jonathan nodded his agreement.

"Super secret spy mission?" Sylvia teased.

"This is such fine weather we're having," Roy replied.

"I wasn't going to ask specifics," Sylvia replied. "Just tell Abby I have that book she wanted to borrow. I'll come by with it sometime."

"When?" Jonathan asked. Roy raised an eyebrow at him, but Jonathan didn't notice.

"Tuesday, at 1:19 pm." They both laughed.

"1:19? Why?" Jonathan asked.

"It seemed like a funny question, so I gave you a funny answer."

Roy paid the money and they grabbed all of the bags and followed Sylvia out to the truck. She went around back and soon came back with a large case of Mountain Dew.

"Where's all your help?" Roy asked. "Usually between here and the hardware store, it's a busy place."

"No one showed up for work today. Or yesterday, for that matter," Sylvia explained. "The only blessing is town has been dead for the past two days as well."

"Everyone go on vacation?" Jonathan asked.

Sylvia shrugged. "No idea. There hasn't even been any mail the past two days."

"No mail?" Roy asked.

"The airfield on the south side of town has been closed for the last two days."

"Doesn't your dad run that airfield?"

"He said he was going on a fishing trip with John from church, but I was surprised he didn't get Gerald or even myself to keep it open. It's not that hard a job."

Roy nodded his agreement. Normally the only things that flew into the airfield were small Cessna airplanes with their mail or packages, of which Geoffrey was now one of the pilots and had reported the same thing. The three of them stood silent for a moment.

Jonathan studied him carefully. "You're thinking something. What's wrong, Captain?" he asked. Sylvia perked up, hearing the title, *Captain*.

"It is very unlike Henry to leave his job and not get Gerald to watch the airfield. And town is a little too empty for my liking."

"You think something's wrong?" Sylvia asked.

"I'm not sure yet," Roy admitted after a moment.

"Lulls like this happen in any town, though," Jonathan argued.

"Yes, but this troubles my heart in a different way," Roy replied. "Unknown to most people, in the last month and a half, nearly thirty people have either disappeared of left the town for one reason or another."

"Really?" Sylvia asked. "Who?"

"Jensens, Old Cartwright and his wife, I haven't even seen John Harrison lately." He turned to Sylvia. "Have you?" She thought for a moment.

"If I have, it escapes me, and that's rare," she said. "My dad did say that he was going on a fishing trip with John, that would at least explain why my dad didn't get him to watch the airfield."

"They could've moved to a different town?" Jonathan asked.

"Trust me...people in this town don't move," Sylvia interjected. Both of them looked to Roy.

"Sylvia, can you help us with some wood from the hardware?"
Sylvia nodded.

"Great, here's what we need. Jonathan, stay and help her load up. I'm going to a walk around town. Something's just not adding up."

He didn't say another word as he wandered away from them, studying everything intently. In all the time he had lived here, Roy had never seen it this empty. He quickly ducked into the store again, grabbing the telephone and dialing the number for Terra's. It rang endlessly until Roy finally hung up the phone.

Roy sighed heavily and stepped out the front door, noticing stones along the little path. He admired them but at the same time, was wary of the new addition. Roy reached down and picked up a light grey stone at the end of the path. The others were rough, while this one was smooth and dense. Roy studied it and was lost in his thoughts. A while later Sylvia and Jonathan came around the corner.

"Everything okay?" Sylvia asked.

"Where did you get these stones?" Roy asked.

"The one in your hand is a mystery to me," Sylvia said. "I found it near my house about a week ago. It looked unusual and kind of cool, so I brought it here." Roy nodded and pondered everything.

"I think there's something going on," Roy concluded. "Sylvia, I think I need to leave Jonathan here with you to help in whatever way he can. Would you be able to bring him home after work?"

"It'll cost you," Sylvia teased.

Roy motioned Jonathan around the corner for a moment.

"What did you find?" Jonathan asked, once they were alone. Roy handed him the smooth rock.

"Watch the coloring of it," Roy instructed. They stared at it, noticing how the grey seemed to shift from a lighter grey to a darker grey.

"Is this what I think it is?" Jonathan asked. Roy nodded.

"It's a Sactaline, but what kind I cannot tell you. I've never seen one like this before."

"What do you think it means?"

"I think it means there's more trouble in this town than we first thought."

4

GEOFFREY STIRRED FROM his slumber more sore than he ever remembered being in his entire life. He opened his eyes, realizing he was laying on a large bed. His mind struggled to make sense of what was happening. Was he asleep in Roy's cabin? Had everything been a dream?

His heart raced as he heard the door open and someone come in the room. Whoever it was sat down in a large chair and was opening some sort of bag.

"Ah yes, thank you, my precious," a voice said. Geoffrey immediately recognized it as Alexander. He carefully peeked over the top of the cover that had been laid over him to see Alexander sitting at a table, relishing in delight at a paper bag. Alexander appeared to not notice that Geoffrey was awake, and continued talking to himself.

"This is how I know my wife loves me." He pulled a note off the bag. "Alexander please enjoy these while you keep an eye on the off-worlder. I'll be back in time for supper." He put the note down. And smiled at the bag again.

"At last! The *Chrunchler!*" He pulled a chip from the bag and studied it intently. It was blueish in color. "The crunchiest, loudest, most awesome chips on the planet...and I get to eat them!" With that he shoved the chip in his mouth. Geoffrey had to cover his ears as a sound similar to that of glass shattering filled the room. Alexander giggled in childish delight as he continued crunching. Geoffrey watched from his spot, wondering if he should say anything. Finally, Geoffrey couldn't contain himself any longer.

"What the heck do they make that chip out of!?" Geoffrey exclaimed. Alexander jumped and yelled out at the same time, sending the rest of the chips scattering all over the room. Geoffrey broke out into laughter.

"Sorry, didn't mean to scare you."

"Oh yeah, sure. I can see now that you and Roy are definitely related!" Alexander exclaimed. Geoffrey helped him pick up the chips.

"Okay, so I meant to scare you," Geoffrey replied. "But that was the best thing I've seen all day." Alexander smiled and chuckled.

"Not hard, when you've been sleeping for so long," Alexander pointed out.

"Can't argue, but that does bring me back to some interesting questions," Geoffrey started. "How long have I been asleep? Where are we exactly? And where is Roy?"

"Question one: You've been asleep for about twelve hours. Question two: you are in the Reno household in the city of Granyon, which is the home of the Chrystarian Knights. Question three : Roy is currently still in his cabin in Vermont, at least as far as I know. The door has disappeared, and therefore, you are stuck doing life with us for the current moment."

"So I wasn't dreaming?"

"Afraid not."

"I remember being in a forest. How did I get here?"

"We flew on the back of a Griffin. We tied you on. It was perfectly safe."

"I see," Geoffrey said, studying the room with a new fascination. "So am I actually in a different world?"

"See for yourself!"

Alexander motioned towards a door that led to a balcony. Geoffrey nervously stepped through the doorway and into the bright sunny day. Buildings and structures were everywhere, and thousands of Griffins streamed through the sky, all with people on them. Geoffrey looked in disbelief as he noticed all the buildings were constructed on platforms that floated in the air. Alexander smiled.

"Don't worry, you'll get used to it."

"I don't know about that," Geoffrey said. "Is this actually real?"

"Of course it's real."

"But I'm wondering which is actually real. Is this real or is back home real?"

"They're both real."

"There must be one that's more real than the other."

"No, they both seem to exist, last I checked," Alexander replied.

"But how is that possible?"

"How should I know?"

"You live here."

"Yeah, but you just asked a question that enters the 'God Realm', as your brother would call it. How it *is*, I don't know because I'm not God. But he *is* God, so he can do anything he wants."

"I suppose," Geoffrey said, thinking for a moment. "Still, doesn't your mind and heart wonder how these things exist? Maybe one came from the other."

"You lost me."

"Maybe this world was created because of something in my world."

"Let me just stop you before you say anything more stupid than what you just said," Alexander said, putting his chips down. "Just imagine you're on a beach...where a beautiful sandcastle stands tall and proud. With your one statement you said, '*Oh what a nice sandcastle. The wind and the waves must have built that. How lovely!*'

34

"But that's-"

"The stupidest thing I've ever heard!" Alexander exclaimed. "This world and *your* world are both created. One did not create the other, because *if* one is created then it is bound by time. If it's bound by time, it could not have created itself. *Logically*, to create either or both worlds, you would have to be *beyond* time in order to set everything in order."

"So you're certain that both this world, and the one I'm from, are real?" Geoffrey asked.

"If they weren't, we wouldn't be having this conversation."

"It just doesn't make sense," Geoffrey complained.

"This isn't about it *'making sense'*. It's about having some faith."

"It seems I have very little of that."

"Perhaps it will grow in the time that you spend here!" a new voice said. They turned to see the source of the voice. A middle height man entered the room. His hair was brown and neatly combed; his beard was nicely groomed. He walked tall and proud and with certainty and conviction. Alexander nodded his respects as the man approached them.

"Who are you?" Geoffrey asked.

The man smiled. "I am Chrystar. Leader of the Kingdom. I have come to encourage and lead the Chrystarians in their fight against the Alliance and the Hentar Knights." He paused and looked directly at Geoffrey. Geoffrey slowly began to feel uncomfortable as it seemed Chrystar was looking right into his soul. "Now it's my turn. Who are you?"

"Geoffrey Van Doren, sir," Geoffrey managed.

"And what does that mean?" Chrystar asked. Geoffrey stared at him blankly. "Who is Geoffrey Van Doren...here." Chrystar touched his heart. Geoffrey couldn't utter a reply.

"What news?" Alexander asked.

"One more thing first." He turned to face Geoffrey. "As far as how both worlds exist, have you not heard that God created the *heavens* and the *earth?*"

"Are you saying this is heaven?" Geoffrey asked.

"No, but the principle is the same," Chrystar said. "But now, to other things! Gideon is currently buried in the library searching for something to help Roy. I am here to help speed your training along! Time is short, and you must have a general knowledge before you are thrown into battle."

"I don't really want to be in a war," Geoffrey admitted.

"You already are. It's time you learn some skill with a blade and a bow. What do you know about them?"

"Nothing."

"Good. Then we're working with a clean slate. Much easier than having to erase and start over-"

"Sorry to interrupt, but I have one more question before we continue with whatever this is," Geoffrey said. Chrystar's eyes were kind and warm and suddenly Geoffrey felt his nerves relax. "I ended up here by accident. Why?"

"Logical question to ask," Chrystar replied. "But do you suppose you really came here by accident? Or were you brought here for such a time as this?" Geoffrey didn't respond, his mind nearly overwhelmed with the implications of what had been said. "You are here because you're supposed to be here. You have much to contribute to the war, you have much to bring to the table. You are capable of much more than you know! And I hope someday you put it to good use."

Geoffrey's mind burned with questions, but was unable to form the words as he looked at the two people in front of him. In just the short time he had seen either of them, it was plain to see that they were as different as night and day, but as he watched them interact, Geoffrey could see that something greater united them.

"Come along! Come along! We haven't got all day!" Chrystar said, motioning them towards the door. Before Geoffrey could fully comprehend what had happened they found themselves in the midst of a great open field which lay just behind the large building they were in. Chrystar and Alexander scurried around the field, already knowing what was going to happen.

"I know this may be a little sudden, but there's a lot to teach you and little time to do it. First thing." Chrystar pulled from a bag a glowing stone like he had seen before. "This is a Sactaline. Very nice, very handy. Stuff can be stored in some of it. Like bolts and uniforms, and now weapons can also be stored. Give that a tap."

Geoffrey tapped it, and in a moment he was dressed in armor with a sword on one side and a crossbow slung on his back. He looked at it in amazement, wondering once again if all of this was a dream.

"Most versatile weapon is your crossbow, so we'll start with that," Chrystar said. "The arrows explode when they hit anything other than a person's skin. The armor you're wearing will deflect a significant amount of direct hits before it's considered destroyed."

They spent several hours running through drill after drill and letting Geoffrey adjust to the strange weapons. For the most part, Geoffrey seemed to be doing well, considering he had never used anything like these before in his life. Alexander ran around almost faster than Geoffrey thought it to be possible as he set up targets everywhere and would occasionally shoot some arrows of his own at Geoffrey.

From there they moved on to working with their swords. Geoffrey proved to be a natural and picked it up faster than even Alexander and Chrystar seemed to expect. They trained until nightfall came, and finally Geoffrey collapsed on a bench, unsure if he would be able to stay awake any longer.

REBELLION

"You're doing well, Geoffrey," Chrystar said. Geoffrey managed a smile at the compliment. "In the morning you will leave with Alexander and Savannah for their mission in Merodia." Geoffrey's face clearly showed his surprise.

"What? I've only started training and you want to send me on a mission?" Geoffrey asked. Chrystar's expression was unchanged, which was both comforting and alarming.

"Yes," Chrystar finally replied. "You must go."

"But why?" Geoffrey asked. "Can't I stay and train a little more at least?"

"No, the time has come and you must go with them."

"I don't understand. Why must I go now?" Geoffrey asked.

"We always send three or more on a mission," Chrystar answered. "Three people can more easily support each other, if one falls down, two can pick him up. It is harder for Lucerine to get a hold on a person's heart if there are two more that are strong in their faith. A cord of three strands is not easily broken."

"That make sense," Geoffrey said.

"Something else is on your mind," Chrystar replied. Geoffrey wanted to refute, but instead a silence came over them.

"What am I supposed to do here?" Geoffrey asked. "I suppose I'm feeling a little overwhelmed by everything that's happened. I was just a postal man yesterday, and now I'm being trained to fight in a war that I know nothing about."

"Your coming here had nothing to do with this war," Chrystar said. "Here you may be a warrior; at home you may be a postal man, but no matter which world you live in, you are the same person inside. So often people put emphasis on the outward appearance that they forget to look further ahead to what really matters. Ultimately, your character is far more

38

important than your *success* in life. I cannot promise that you will come back from the war that you are now heading into, but the question is, will you take a stand?"

Geoffrey thought for a moment, long and hard. A stirring in his heart and his mind seemed to burn with new energy that he had never felt before. Confidence came over him.

"Yes, I'll fight with you," Geoffrey said. "Though I still don't quite understand what I'm doing." They chuckled.

"In time things will become clear," Chrystar said. "Sorry for the late hour, but I've got to get going. Good luck on your mission tomorrow. I must be off!" They watched as Chrystar walked away. He and Alexander started walking back to the Reno house.

"How are you feeling about everything?" Alexander asked.

"Still not sure which way is up, but I think I'll be okay," Geoffrey responded.

"If you're anything like Roy, you'll do just fine. Better than fine, actually."

"What's my brother like in this world?" Geoffrey asked.

"He's a good leader, a cunning warrior, and most importantly a good friend and husband to my sister. I'm glad to know him."

"I have the feeling he's very different from what I knew a couple of days ago."

"He probably is, but not in a bad way."

"What about Chrystar?" Geoffrey asked.

"What do you think of him?" Alexander countered.

Geoffrey thought for a moment. "I'm not sure. I trust him, though. Strange as it is. I only met him earlier today."

"Chrystar has the ability to see potential in us that we don't see in ourselves. He clearly sees something in you that he likes."

39

"What do you think it is?"

"Not sure, but I am glad that you don't snore nearly as bad as Roy does." Geoffrey laughed.

"I'm glad of that, too. I'm not sure how Abby puts up with it."

"She's blinded by love," Alexander replied. They both laughed. Soon they found themselves back in the roomy apartment that Alexander and Savannah called their home.

Savannah had returned an hour earlier and had dinner made for all of them when they walked in. They said a prayer and ate the food which Geoffrey didn't exactly recognize. That being said, it tasted fine in the stomach. They retreated to the living room afterwards where they traded stories and tales for nearly an hour.

Geoffrey marveled at everything around him, starting to look at it in a new way. As strange as it was, and as much as he might feel like he was going insane, these two people were already making him feel like family.

He watched them in amusement as they most certainly seemed like an odd couple.

"How was your meeting?" Alexander finally asked.

"Most of it was taking some flight time on the Dreygar," Savannah answered. "They fly very different from Griffins."

"Different in what way?" Alexander inquired.

"They feel more stiff. More forced in their movements."

"Harder to fly?" Geoffrey asked.

"I just hope I don't have to fly it in combat conditions."

"With any luck we'll get to Merodia, find this 'Trace' person and get out of there," Alexander said.

"Speaking of which, we should head to bed now. I want to be going by first light," Savannah told them. Reluctantly, they stopped the good conversation and headed to their rooms. Geoffrey lay staring at the window

40

and the lights that shone, wondering about what tomorrow might hold.

5

IT WAS NEARLY MIDNIGHT when Roy heard a car door outside the cabin. With the exception of himself and Abby, everyone else was already asleep for the night. Abby was upstairs, waiting to see if they would hear from someone else anytime soon.

They had fixed the hole in the wall, and by the time supper was over, all twenty-one members of the A-Team who were present had found a place on the couches or the floor and had fallen asleep. Amid all the blankets and pillows strewn about the living room, Roy could hardly even walk through his own house.

He heard the car pull away as Jonathan came in through the front door.

"I was starting to think we had lost you," Roy teased. "How is Sylvia?"

"Just fine," Jonathan replied.

"Just fine," Roy teased with a smile. Jonathan tried to hide his own.

"I'm not talking!"

"You don't have to, I can see it in your eyes. Did you have a good afternoon?"

Now Jonathan smiled widely. "Yes, I did. I tried not to make it too obvious that I didn't have a clue about what she was talking about, or the fact that I didn't know what kind of food we were eating."

"I'm sure you played your cards just right. Find anything?"

"Yes, a great deal." Jonathan reached for one of the bags he had brought.

It was taller than the rest and a fair deal heavier. He dumped the contents on the table. Roy immediately recognized nearly twenty Sactalines that were identical to the one he had discovered earlier in the day. Roy picked one up in his hand and studied it intently.

"Any clues about them?" Roy asked.

"Nothing obvious," Jonathan said. "I've recalled all my training on the matter, and I can't ever remember anything about a grey Sactaline. They were hidden everywhere, and places you wouldn't think to look. One was on top of the water tower, the next would be in the trash can, or on someone's desk as a paper weight. How can you explain this?"

"I can't," Roy admitted, setting it on the table. "Unless some other gateway has been discovered between the worlds, I'm not sure how to explain it." They fell silent for a minute or two, each of them lost in their own thoughts. After another moment, Jonathan smiled, seeing a bottle of Cabin Juice. He gleefully snatched it up and broke the seal.

"Did everyone enjoy the rest?" Jonathan asked.

"It's still in the truck," Roy replied.

Jonathan's smile grew. "I know what I'm having to drink with breakfast!" Roy chuckled.

Then, the door to the upstairs opened and Abby appeared at the top of the stairs. "Roy, come quick!"

Roy and Jonathan both came as fast as they could without waking everybody. They clamored up the stairs and followed Abby to the wall, which was patched up with plywood. Abby held a finger to her lips. They remained silent, finally hearing what Abby had wanted them to hear.

From inside the cabin they could hear the rustling of leaves and heavy footsteps stomping noisily through the forest. Abby motioned that they should leave. They gently closed the door, then tiptoed down the stairs again and moved out to the front porch.

43

"Who do you think that was?" Jonathan asked, easing into one of the wooden deck chairs.

"I have no idea, but if we can hear them, there's a good chance they can hear us," Abby replied, sitting in the seat beside him. "There were two other voices earlier, trying to figure out why there was so much burnt vegetation."

"We'd better be careful who and what goes on in that upstairs room until further notice," Roy stated. The others nodded their agreement. "This is starting to get confusing." They quickly filled Abby in on everything that Jonathan had discovered in town.

"The mysteries grows," Abby said.

"Normally, I love a good mystery, but this one's starting to wear on me a little," Roy admitted.

"I'm sure it'll all work out, hon."

"I'm sure it will too, but we're stuck here, and Geoffrey is stuck there, and we still haven't heard from anybody."

"That's about to change," a voice said. Immediately, all of them searched for the source of the voice in the darkness around the porch. Then they all remained quiet for a few moments, waiting for the voice to speak to them again.

"Is anybody there?" the voice asked again. "Hello?"

"Hi," Roy hesitantly responded. "Who's this?"

"It's me, Gideon."

"Where are you?" Abby asked.

"In my house. Where else would I be?" Gideon replied. "You must have your Sactalines nearby. I figure that's the only reason we can talk."

"So you are talking through the Sactalines?" Jonathan asked.

"Yes, just like I would on an assignment." Gideon answered. Roy quickly grabbed his Sactalines and tapped all of them. He was immediately adorned in his uniform, with armor, weapons and Sactalines embedded in the chest as they always were.

"It's good to hear from you, Gideon."

"Likewise. I've been briefed on what happened. How is Evelyn?"

"Peacefully sleeping," Abby answered. "She may not show her nervousness about being stuck here, but I can see it."

"I'm sure. Take good care of her until I can get to you guys, or vise-versa. Also, let her know the girls and I are doing just fine!"

"We will," Roy replied. "How's Geoffrey doing?"

"I haven't gotten a chance to meet him ye—"

"He's doing just fine Roy, don't worry," a voice interrupted. Roy and the others were taken aback as they recognized Savannah's voice. "Glad you made it back to this world."

"Actually, I didn't."

"What?"

"We're still in my cabin."

"How can I hear you?" Savannah asked.

"I'm not quite sure. Apparently Sactalines work in both worlds."

"This is all very freaky just so you know!" Geoffrey's voice exclaimed.

"How are you doing, Geoffrey?"

"I'm still alive, which is good, but all of *this* is threatening to push me over the edge. I still have no idea what it is we're flying on, and we're currently headed towards some city called Merriment."

"Merodia," they heard Alexander correct.

"Whatever," Geoffrey replied. "This does explain a lot about why you've been hard to get a hold of recently."

"If it's any consolation, I'm glad I don't have to keep this a secret from you anymore," Roy said.

"Right now, I'm surprised you could keep it a secret at all."

"It wasn't easy," Roy replied. "Gideon, do you happen to have any secrets on how we might get this door to reappear?"

"I'm afraid not," Gideon answered. "My father never saw the door again. However, Chrystar has brought me to a part of the libraries that I've never known existed before. It has a lot of interesting stuff in it."

"Interesting?"

"Your little cabin has been around for a long time. I have some testaments of off-worlders coming through your cabin...the oldest of which is one thousand years old."

"Anything on the door, though?"

"Nothing. It actually appears that you may be the first person to truly traverse both worlds simultaneously. I have begun finding a few references to different ways into the world, but nothing for certain, yet."

"Chrystar once told me there were three ways into the world," Roy replied.

"I'll have to look into it. Keep in mind though that even if I find it here, I'm not sure how we're going to find it in your world."

"Noted. Hey, have you ever heard anything about grey Sactalines?"

"Grey? Can't say that I have."

"My town is covered in them, and I'm not sure what to do about it."

"Be careful. That's my best advice." There was a moment of silence. "I've got some very serious reading to do, so I will check out for the moment. Let me know if anything happens."

"We're going to be dropping our Sactalines as we're approaching Merodia," Savannah said.

"Good thinking," Roy complimented. The talking ceased and Roy remained deep in thought.

"What are you thinking, Roy?" Abby asked.

"I'm not even sure right now."

They sat in silence for a moment until the silence was unexpectedly shattered by screeching soaring through the sky above them. Within seconds they had all risen to their feet and looked into the darkness. Chills ran up and down their spines as the shadows of Dreygar's passed overhead of the cabin.

"I don't believe it!" Jonathan said, studying the sky. "There's ten of them."

"How'd they get in this world?" Abby asked. They both looked to Roy, who looked as confused at they felt.

"I'm not sure, but they're headed straight for town," Roy concluded. "Get the others up. We've got a rescue mission."

Abby and Jonathan ran back inside, quickly waking everyone. Roy grabbed a flashlight from the counter and walked around the backside of the cabin. He picked up a large chest and carried it inside. By the time he reached the front door, everyone was up and standing in line.

"Sorry for the late hour. What we know is that we've just seen Dreygars in this world. They may be heading towards Granville."

"What for?" Evelyn asked.

"I don't know, but we're going to treat this like a rescue mission."

"We don't have any weapons," one of the men protested. Roy opened the chest which was filled to the brim with Sactalines. They all gasped in amazement.

"One of my contingency plans," Roy replied. Moments later, they were all in uniforms with weapons and armor. "Unlike home, we don't have a nearly endless supply of bolts, so if you have to take a shot, make it count." He looked over the group again. "Jonathan can ride with me in the cab. Abigail, if you could tell everyone what they need to know, I would be very appreciative. Everyone, to the truck!"

They ran out to the truck and everyone jumped into the back of it. Roy tore out of the driveway and made it to the road in record time.

"What do you suppose they're going to do with everyone?" Jonathan asked.

"I don't think I even have a guess at this point," Roy admitted. "I know I usually have a plan, but this is that time when we make the plan up as we go."

"I hope Sylvia's alright," Jonathan said.

Roy sighed heavily. "I just hope we make it in time to figure out what's going on."

6

GEOFFREY TRIED HIS best to not look at the vast ocean spreading out below him. In the fading sunlight he could see nothing except endless amounts of water. He now rode atop a horrifyingly large creature which was called a Dreygar.

"How fast does this thing go?" Geoffrey asked. As much as he was trying to be grumpy about the entire situation, he couldn't deny that he was intrigued by all the new things around him, even if at the same time it was a little overwhelming. All three of them sat casually on top of the Dreygar. Alexander and Savannah had both gone to great lengths to convince him that their uniforms were magnetic, but even still in all his movements Geoffrey was remaining cautious.

"By the mathematics in your world I couldn't even begin to guess," Alexander said. "I'm not even sure we have specific measurements for something like this."

"Mostly it's measured in time increments," Savannah replied. "An hour is called a *ferlin*. It's rather an old term and doesn't get used to much except by pilots."

"You said Roy knows how to fly these?"

"Better than I do," Savannah answered. "He's the best pilot we've ever had." Geoffrey gave a baffled expression and Savannah caught it. "How well do you know your brother?"

REBELLION

"He had become pretty distant after everything that had happened with our parents. Then for a while he didn't talk to me at all. Then one day I did hear from him, and it's been an improving situation ever since."

"What do you think caused his change of heart?" Alexander asked.

"Knowing what I know now, I would say I think it was this place that changed it," Geoffrey admitted. "And now after everything, I find out that he's a pilot, too. Something in common, you know?" They both nodded but Geoffrey still felt like it was something they didn't understand.

They talked and chatted for a while before running through more drills and rehearsing what might be said when they landed in Merodia. They fell silent and the sun vanished from the sky. Geoffrey's anxiety grew more with each second that passed.

"Do you feel confident?" Alexander asked.

"No."

"Good. Overconfidence will kill you long before anything else will."

"That's not very comforting," Geoffrey replied. Alexander smirked.

"Perhaps not, but it's true. I wouldn't worry to much, just like your brother, you're catching on amazingly fast." Geoffrey smiled at the notion.

They fell into silence again and within a minute a dim glow appeared on the water. As they approached Geoffrey felt as though he would never be able to put into words what he was seeing.

The dim glow grew to be a city larger than any he had ever laid eyes on. Buildings rose untold distances into the sky, far above them. Dreygars filled the sky and the glow of Sactalines illuminated the entire city. With all the Sactalines glowing, Geoffrey couldn't help but notice that it looked like any other city from the real world.

They entered the massive city, which Geoffrey noticed was anchored in the water. The buildings were made of a dark black rock, which sparkled and shimmered due to the moisture that collected on the side of the building. Alexander had tried to explain that the people of Merodia somehow extracted all their drinking water from the surface of the rock. Buildings and bridges appeared to have been arranged in no particular order.

"Where are we headed?" Geoffrey asked.

"I'm not entirely sure. The message said to get to Merodia and find 'Trace'," Alexander reminded. "Look for something that's different or out of place."

They flew for several minutes, now completely swallowed by the city. Geoffrey marveled at the buildings and architecture. The longer they flew, the more he began to enjoy himself.

They all cried out at once as the Dreygar lurched sharply to the left and descended at a rapid pace. Everyone's hands moved to their weapons, ready to fire them at a moment's notice. A few seconds later they relaxed, observing no threats on the horizon.

Just when they had relaxed, it happened again, this time veering to the right, down one street and then left down another. In front of them the city gave way to a massive forest with rivers snaking its way through it. The water glowed iridescent green and was completely still.

"Be ready for anything," Savannah warned. "I have no idea what's going on."

"The Dreygar seems to have a mind of his own," Geoffrey observed.

"I've given up on trying to give it directions for the moment," Savannah replied.

"Where do you think it's taking us?" Alexander asked.

"That building straight ahead," Geoffrey said. A new line of buildings had appeared on the horizon and each one appeared to be identical to the other.

"Why that building?"

"Look at the shinny thing—"

"Sactaline."

"Right, Sactaline. On top of every building is a red Sactaline, except the one straight ahead. That one is orange." Alexander and Savannah strained their eyes but couldn't see anything on the building clearly for several minutes.

"I do believe you have a ridiculous knack for observation, like your brother," Alexander complimented again. Geoffrey smiled, as they let the Dreygar take them closer to the building. They descended lower and lower, until they could finally see an opening in the rock building nearly fifty feet up off the ground. The building grew even more enormous in size, and in comparison Geoffrey felt like an ant that was about to be squashed.

They were swallowed by a darkened opening. Once inside they found they were flying through a complex tunnel system which was dotted with white Sactalines and torches.

Then all at once, they were overcome with light, brilliant white light. Squinting, they took in their new surroundings. They were now in an assembly area of some kind. How large it was and how far the area stretched in all directions, Geoffrey couldn't hope to guess.

The walls and ceiling were made out of the same stone that the outside of the building had been, except that it was white, with light blue veins running through it. The floor, on the other hand, was made of a red rock. Both walls and floors were polished, reflecting any light that was in the room.

The Dreygar slowed and casually landed in the middle of the great expanse. Geoffrey followed the other's lead as Alexander and Savannah began dismounting.

"What now?" he heard Alexander whisper. They didn't have a moment to do anything as hundreds, if not thousands, of armed soldiers came pouring into the space, filling it. The people at the front drew their swords, while the others, if they had a clear sight, raised their bows. Savannah and Alexander exchanged glances, but neither one seemed to know what to do.

Throwing caution to the wind, Geoffrey stepped forward.

"You're all a bunch of imbeciles!" Geoffrey yelled. Savannah and Alexander were clearly taken back by his tone as he strode up to the tallest of the group. "Is this any way to treat people like us?" The soldier looked frightened and opened his mouth but no words came out.

"What is your name, soldier?" Geoffrey yelled.

"Ta-Tammer, sir!"

"Well, *Ta-Tammer,* you tell us what this is all about, or I will have you dragged out of here by your big toe and thrown into that flipping big ocean! Do I make myself clear?"

"Yes, sir," Tammer replied. "We were sent to escort you to the meeting chamber."

"And it takes ten million of you to do it?!" Geoffrey yelled. Out of the corner of his eye he could see Alexander and Savannah trying to keep a straight face.

"No-no-no, sir. Apologies. I'll have a small group of five lead you there immediately!" Tammer said, his voice getting higher and higher with each word he spoke.

"Thank you!" Geoffrey exclaimed. He looked over all the people. "At least *this* guy knows how to do a job!" With amazing speed, the large number of soldiers dwindled to five. Tammer stood before them, trembling.

"I'll gladly take you to the Minister now," Tammer managed.

"Thank you, fine sir," Geoffrey replied. Tammer's face displayed confusion at the change in tone. "Sorry for yelling. I was just trying to get to the point. Could you give me and my comrades here just a moment to collect our thoughts?"

"Yes, of course! We'll wait for you." Tammer and his men pulled back nearly fifty feet. Geoffrey turned to Alexander and Savannah.

"That was frightening," Alexander said, smiling from ear to ear. "The last time I heard a scolding like that was from my drill Sergeant during training."

"Why were you getting scolded?" Geoffrey asked.

Alexander's face hardened, while Savannah's lit up as if recalling a pleasant memory.

"We don't have time for that," Alexander said, plainly.

"Legendary," Savannah replied. "Ask Roy sometime." Alexander started to protest but Savannah held a hand up. "We'd better get going." They began walking to the soldiers waiting for them.

"Who are we supposed to meet here?" Geoffrey whispered.

"Someone named 'Trace'," Savannah replied.

They reached Tammer and his men, who now stood at attention. Geoffrey assumed the lead in order to keep the charade.

"If you'll follow me, the Minister has been expecting you."

They all exchanged glances, uncertainty coming over them like a crashing wave. Geoffrey still held himself high as they began their journey through the maze of halls and passages.

Each hall or passage held the same majestic poise that the first had, with the only real difference being the color of the rock that made up the floor or walls. Several grand staircases and bridges led to other levels each more exquisite than the last.

They lost track of time and direction as they descended through several levels and entered a hall that was more plain and simple then the rest. At the entrance to the hall, five soldiers stood guard. Behind them a plain grey stone hall loomed. Though there were plenty of Sactalines shining brightly, the stone in this hall did not reflect the light the way the others had.

They were marched past the guards without a word being spoken and ushered to the very end, where a single set of double doors stood. The doors were opened, and they were led into a large, but cozy meeting room, with a desk at the head and a long curved table and chairs facing the desk at the front.

A window was in the far left wall, giving a breathtaking view of the city. From here they could see that they had descended to nearly sea level. Waves crashed upon great walls that formed a barrier from the sea.

Tammer bowed to them. "The Minister will be with you shortly. Sorry again for the greeting you received."

"It's nothing to worry about. Sorry I scared you," Geoffrey replied.

"I hope you understand, sir, that I could get in trouble for scaring you so badly and to upset someone like the Minister may mean I will lose my life."

"I will put in a good word with the Minister, I assure you," Geoffrey said. Tammar seemed satisfied and left, leaving them alone in the room. All three of them collapsed into the chairs.

"Look at the bright side. We're meeting all the important people in Merodia," Savannah said.

"I can't say I expected to meet the Minister," Alexander replied. "This should be interesting."

"What's our story?" Geoffrey asked.

"I don't know," Alexander replied. "I'm intrigued that they are apparently expecting us."

"Or did they mistake us for someone else?" Savannah asked. None of them had an answer and they remained silent, thinking about their situation.

"Be whoever we need to be," Alexander said. "We cannot possibly know what will be said when the Minister comes through that door...whatever it is, roll with it."

"Yes, sir," Geoffrey said, growing more nervous as the time dragged on. Though it felt like an hour, it was likely only a few minutes before a knock came and a person entered.

"Alexander!" the person greeted. Surprise flooded over both Alexander and Savannah's face. He was mid-height with longer black hair that was parted and combed. He wore a long black robe and wore no weapons that they could see.

"Cyrus!" Alexander exclaimed. In an instant Cyrus embraced him and in turn, shook hands with Savannah and Geoffrey.

"It's good to see all of you. I'm assuming by now you two lovebirds are married?"

"Yes, we are," Savannah said, forcing a smile, but Geoffrey could tell there was an interesting story here.

"Glad to hear. Sorry I couldn't come to the wedding...even if I was invited, I think we both know I wouldn't have been able to come," Cyrus said. He turned to face Geoffrey.

"And to my other guest I would like to introduce myself. I am Cyrus Reno, Alexander's brother. And you are?"

"Roy's brother, Geoffrey Van Doren," Geoffrey replied. Cyrus's eyes seemed to light up, but whether it was a good thing or not Geoffrey couldn't tell.

"It's an honor to meet you." He turned to everyone. "I know you must have a lot of questions and have traveled far. Please have a seat, and if there is anything that you would like to refresh yourself, I can call for it in a moment. Not that it will get here right away, but you get the point."

They all took a seat in the luxurious chairs. Geoffrey watched the other three intently.

"So how have you been?" Alexander asked, awkwardly.

"I've been quite well, thank you. What business brings you to my city on one of my Dreygars?" Cyrus asked.

"Your Dreygars?" Alexander asked.

Cyrus smiled. "I had a set of three dozen trained and set free, and then tipped off another friend of mine who is a friend of the Kingdom to catch them," Cyrus said proudly. "I needed them to be found in order for you to easily gain access into Merodia. You probably already know, but Merodia is ordered to shoot any Griffin it sees."

"Because of you?" Savannah asked.

"Because of the Alliance." Cyrus replied. "I don't make the rules, but I do have to enforce them."

"I see. So you've cleverly designed a method to get us here. Why?" Geoffrey asked.

Cyrus seemed to consider his reply carefully. "I've got many interests and not all of them are able to be discussed at this particular moment. The Kingdom received a letter from a man named 'Trace'. I am Trace. Many of the people in my city know me as Trace or the Minister, not Cyrus."

"Why the secrecy?" Alexander asked.

"The Senate passed a war protection law. Stating that the Hentarian Knights and generals of the Alliance could form an alias to protect their identity."

"I never heard about that," Savannah said.

"It was kept very hush-hush. In my opinion, it was really a rather sketchy procedural document. But it protects me from discovery."

"I suppose that is a good thing," Alexander said after a moment. "I am glad to know that you are alive and well. Though a war may stand between us, you are still family to me."

"Likewise," Cyrus replied.

REBELLION

Geoffrey mulled over everything carefully, uncertainty clouding the situation.

"I will not forget what you did for me when this war started. Saving those civilians. I once again ask how the three young ladies, we rescued are doing?" Cyrus asked.

"Yeah, about that...they have never heard of a Cyrus Reno in their entire life. I do hope one of these days that you tell me who these girls are to you, but in answer to your question: They're doing quite fine, they've been taken in by Gideon and Evelyn and most likely they will, when they are old enough join the fight...against you...the Hentarian Knights and the Alliance."

"I'm glad to hear it," Cyrus said.

"I've hardly met you, but I have no idea if I should trust you or not!" Geoffrey exclaimed.

"We have an interesting history," Alexander admitted. "Cyrus, my brother, is a Hentarian Knight. The highest ranking warriors in the Alliance."

"And the Alliance is the bad guys?"

"Yes, that's correct," Alexander replied.

"Even if he is your brother, the situation seems a little too chummy for my liking," Geoffrey said.

"You do what you have to," Savannah said. "Anytime we know he's near a target we're going to be attacking, or if we see him in battle, we look the other way and get the people around him instead."

"Yes, and the A-Team is much harder to catch," Cyrus admitted. "All through this war, my men haven't been able to definitively pin down a single one of your people."

"I guess you'll just have to step up your game, brother," Alexander said, seeming to be enjoying himself. He put his hands behind his head and let both of his feet onto the desk.

"The bigger problem is that the A-Team is forbidden to be captured by deadly force," Cyrus explained.

"Why?" Geoffrey asked.

Cyrus hesitated. "Lucerine, leader of the Hentar and the Alliance, is adamant that all of you be captured alive. I wish I could tell you why, but I simply do not know." They were silent for a moment.

"Alright, you might as well jut tell me," Alexander started. "How did you come to be the Minister of this place?"

"I completed some important missions, and as a reward Lucerine told me that I could name anything and keep it as my own. I told him that I wished only for the city of Merodia and controlling interest in the natural resources. I was granted my request, and now I work out of here more than I work out of Bruden."

"I see," Alexander replied. He sunk back into his chair, seeming to be carefully thinking about everything. "So, *Trace*, what are we here for?"

"If you would please follow me, I will be glad to explain everything in better detail, once I give you a tour." With that, Cyrus got up and they followed him out of the office.

7

ROY DROVE AS FAST as he could, while still keeping the truck on the road. The road twisted and turned, and at times the lights didn't shine all the way around the corner. Roy had driven this road enough times that he could probably do it blindfolded.

Everyone in the back didn't seem to mind the driving too much; most of them were having so much fun actually being permitted to go into town. Jonathan on the other hand, was white knuckled as he clung to anything he thought was solid enough to provide safety.

Roy rounded the next bend in the road and then panicked by what he saw in front of them. At the next corner, the road was blocked by twenty Alliance soldiers with weapons at the ready. Jonathan saw it, too, but didn't get a chance to say anything as Roy killed the lights and veered off to the left and onto a small two-track.

"Where's this go?" Jonathan asked. Roy put the truck in park and turned it off.

"I have no idea," Roy admitted, getting out of the truck. The others were silent as Abby climbed out.

"What's going on?" Abby asked.

"Soldiers on the road. Alliance soldiers," Roy answered. A hush came over them.

"What do you think they're doing?"

60

"How did they even get here?"

"Maybe there's a way back?"

Roy held up a hand to silence them.

"Evelyn, do you know where the Alliance keeps their Sactalines on their persons?"

"The Kingdom has them on the chest, obviously," she quickly replied. "The Alliance has most of them on the wrist guard."

Roy considered the options for a moment.

"What are you thinking, hon?" Abigail asked him.

"If we show up at the soldiers dressed like this, it'll be lights out real quick. And if we go in gun's blazing, one of them no doubt will have time to call for help," Roy started.

"What's a gun?" one of the other men asked.

Roy continued. "The best option, and I know it is a crazy one, is misdirection."

"What kind of misdirection?" Evelyn asked.

"There are a lot of things they might not know about this world, so we're going to exploit that. Get ready to make some noise, we're going to be a bunch of wild teenagers. Everyone take off your armor and your uniforms, and leave the Sactalines in the bed of the truck. Jonathan please pass out a bottle of Cabin Juice to everyone."

Everyone followed his orders and within a couple of minutes they were in their normal clothing."What's the plan?" Jonathan asked.

"I'm going to pull up to the soldiers. We're drunk, wild and crazy. When I stop, we'll jump them. When you do, tap all of their Sactalines. If it works, we'll be able to disarm our opponents in a matter of seconds. Then we'll see what we do after that."

Everyone climbed back into the truck and Roy started the engine again.

"Jonathan, feel free to hit that black button on the radio."

"The one you told me not to touch earlier?"

"Yep." Jonathan pushed it and then jumped back and covered his ears as rock music began playing through the speakers.

"Good heavens! What is that?"

"Music in my world," Roy answered. "Not what I usually listen to, but it'll be fitting this time." He leaned out the window. "Everyone ready?" They cheered and raised their bottles of Mountain Dew. "Hang on tight!"

Roy turned the volume on the radio all the way up and then threw the truck into reverse. He pressed the pedal to the floor, sending them careening backward at a frightening pace up the two track. Roy whipped the truck around as they reached the road.

The front end of the truck swung around, and Roy quickly threw the truck into forward and pressed the pedal to the floor. The tires squealed as they were launched forward. Everyone in the back, cheered enthusiastically as they sped toward the Alliance troops.

At the last possible moment Roy brought the truck to a screeching halt and slid it sideways. As planned, Roy and everyone else jumped out at the soldiers. With surprising ease, they were able to tap the soldiers Sactalines and easily overpower them, once their armor and weapons were away. Within twenty seconds the entire group had been disarmed and were being tied up.

"That was fun! Let's do that again!" Abby exclaimed.

"Are you serious?" Jonathan asked.

"It reminded me of the adrenaline rush me and my brothers use to get when we were blowing caves." They laughed and let their victory settle for a minute.

"Alright, back to business. Uniforms and armor. Now," Roy said. They all found their Sactalines and were immediately adorned in their things again. "Victor, Norah, and David, keep an eye on these men, while the rest of us go on ahead. Let us know if there's anything unusual."

"What are the rest of you going to do?" Victor asked.

"We're heading into the town and we'll see what we see," Roy replied.

"Be careful, alright?" Victor said, embracing Abby for a moment.

"We always are, Dad," Abby replied.

They piled in the truck and started heading into town, this time turning the radio off. A few minutes later, they pulled off the road, behind the first house they came to. They all climbed out and assembled around Roy.

"Go in easy, don't make noise, and don't shoot unless you have to," Roy instructed. "Abigail and I will take our group down the middle of the street. Jonathan, stay on the left side, and David, you're the new leader since Savannah is currently not here, you head up the right side."

They spread out and slowly began advancing through the town, which now appeared to be nothing more than a ghost town. Every building was silent and still. A light would be on, in some houses even the TV would still be going, but as they checked each of them they found no one to be home.

"There are signs of struggle in all of these houses," Abigail pointed out.

"There's some blood in the house over here," David called over the Sactaline.

"Have you found anybody?"

"Not a soul."

They continued through the town, passing house after house and finding the same thing in all of them. They reached the town square where they could now see a dozen Sactalines placed in plain sight. They all studied them with fascination as these ones seemed to be two colors at the same time, red and green.

"What are these?" Abigail asked. "I've never seen anything like them before."

"I wish I knew," Roy answered. "Search every building. There has to be

63

some clue as to what happened." They spread out and began a thorough search of all the buildings. Unlike the houses they had passed, each of the business doors were destroyed and the shelves were emptied. In most of the buildings there wasn't even a piece of furniture to be bought.

"Sylvia's store is licked clean," Jonathan reported. "We should check her house, though."

"Do you think hers would be any different than all the others?" Abby asked.

"She lives outside of the town borders, off the main road a little bit. There's a chance she got missed. She may have the answers we need."

"Check it out. The rest of us are going to investigate the town more."

The minutes passed slowly as they carefully studied everything. It appeared as if Dreygars had landed and people had been pulled towards them, likely to be taken somewhere else.

Their attention was diverted as a Tantine arrow flew through the air, lighting up the night. It missed Roy's team, but hit the building nearby. The entire building went up in a tremendous explosion.

They ducked for cover, frantically searching for the source of the single arrow that had been fired. A few seconds later, an endless stream of arrows raced towards them. In an instant Roy and his group drew their swords and blocked a good amount of the arrows, while the rest of them hit their armor and were deflected.

David's team fired towards their new enemy, taking out several and grabbing the attention of the soldiers which were appearing throughout the town. The town was lit up in flashes of flying arrows and explosions as both sides exchanged fire.

The familiar call of Dreygars filled the sky, and with it came more firepower as those riding let their own arrows fly through the air. Roy and his team held their ground, taking cover wherever they could.

64

"Roy, the center of town, where those strange sactalines are, is untouched by everything. The arrows seem to vanish as soon as they reach that one area!" David reported. Roy and Abby both watched, concluding that he was right. The red and green sactalines seemed to have some kind of special abilities that was shielding the area from damage.

"David, hold your ground with your team and try to give us cover. My team is going in!" Before anything else could be said, Roy and his team darted out of their hiding spots and began sprinting towards the center of the town. They leveled their bows at several soldiers, each arrow finding its marks.

They entered the large circle of Sactalines, finding that for a moment the world spun, as if they were passing through to another world. Instead, they were looking at the center of the town, seeing several Dreygars filled with people, and surrounding each of the Dreygars were soldiers and Hentarian Knights.

The Hentarian Knights rushed towards them. Roy drew his sword and fended off a ferocious attack by one Hentar Knight. The others were quickly engaged in intense duels, all the while the rest of the soldiers focused their energy on getting aboard the Dreygars, which took off moment's later.

"David, you're not going to believe this. Everyone! Grab the Sactalines!" Roy yelled to whoever of his team might hear. A few members grabbed the red and green sactalines and shoved them in their pockets. At once the bubble they had been in was illuminated and everyone in the town could see the giant Dreygars as they began taking off.

David and his men fired a volley of bolts towards their enemies, hitting the armor on several Dreygars, but failing to get them out of the sky. A number more were fired directly at the Hentar Knights, with many of them falling.

REBELLION

Roy moved his limbs effortlessly, easily blocking the attacks by their enemies. The Dreygars were climbing higher into the sky, moving towards the north and would soon be lost from sight. Roy dropped down and swung his foot in a circle, the move surprised the Hentar Knight who staggered after not hitting Roy's blade. Roy's foot swept his opponents legs from under him. The Hentar Knight fell, his hit his head on the ground, and went unconscious.

More arrows lit up the town as more Alliance troops rushed out of the woods to attack them. "Hang onto something!" Roy yelled. He aimed his bow at the water tower and let the arrow loose. It struck the tower with incredible speed, a tidal wave cascading to the ground. Roy kept a hold onto the Hentarian Knight who was unconscious and prepared for impact.

The tidal wave struck them all, flushing them all the way back through the town. The wave subsided, having carried them all the way to the truck. They carefully climbed to their feet, able to easily round up and bind the Alliance soldiers.

"Everyone here?" Roy asked. Slowly all of his people began to rise. "David, Jonathan? You still here?"

"Affirmative!" David responded.

"I'm here, too," Jonathan said. "I just got to town...or the lake, I'm not sure which it is." Roy and Abby both shrugged their shoulders.

"Is everything alright with you?" Roy asked.

"I found Sylvia," Jonathan answered. "She's badly injured. They must have thought she was as good as dead and not bothered with her. I don't want to carry her farther than I need to, though."

"Stay where you are and we'll be over with the truck in a minute or two."

"Copy."

"Who did we capture?" Abby asked, coming over to Roy.

TYLER SVEC

"A Hentar Knight," Roy replied. "Between him and Sylvia we should be able to get some answers." Abby knelt down and tapped the Satalines, taking away all the armor and weapons that were on the person. They both jumped in surprise as the Hentar Knight was revealed to be a young woman with long dark brown wavy hair. Roy and Abby exchanged glances.

"Everyone in the truck! Grab every Sactaline you see. We have a lot to figure out."

8

CYRUS HANDED THEM a couple of smaller Sactalines, and Geoffrey knew immediately what they were supposed to do. They tapped them and were adorned in new clothes, however their weapons were no longer at their side. Their new clothes were beautifully made and filled with the bright colors of Merodia.

"Don't worry, you can still access all your weapons at any point by thinking them, but I would argue that they are not needed right now. You've been given diplomatic Sactalines. You'll be able to follow me anywhere now without raising any suspicion. As is custom, everyone will leave us alone as soon as I give the word."

"Thank you for the upgraded wardrobe, brother," Alexander replied jovially. "What does my wife think? Do I look good?"

"You look quite handsome, my dear," Savannah replied. They went back and forth for several seconds, complimenting each other. Geoffrey on the other hand, felt like he was dressed in the finest garments he had ever seen and was afraid of doing anything, for fear of messing it up.

Cyrus opened the door and they swiftly made their way to the left, going down an enormous staircase of granite. They continued on in silence for nearly ten minutes, descending level after level until Geoffrey had no idea what level they were on anymore.

Geoffrey studied Cyrus as they walked, unable to tell if he was giving them the truth, or if only part of it was the truth, or if all of it was a lie. With everything Cyrus had arranged in order to bring them here, Geoffrey couldn't help but wonder what Cyrus was actually up to.

They came to a large black door built into an outcropping of rock. Cyrus looked at them and flashed a proud smile as he threw the door open.

"Stop number one," Cyrus stated as he welcomed them through the doorway. Geoffrey's breath was taken away by everything he was saw. "Welcome, my friends, to Merodia, the Sactaline mining capital of the world!"

Alexander and Savannah were as much in awe as Geoffrey was. Slowly they stepped out onto a glass hallway. Below them as far as the eye could see, thousands of buildings filled the ocean floor. The water all around was filled with the light. Geoffrey looked above, not seeing even a hint of the surface.

"How deep are we?" Geoffrey asked.

"By now? Probably about half a mile," Cyrus answered.

"So this is what the mines of Merodia are like?" Alexander asked.

"Yes, although technically the term 'mines' is not correct," Cyrus explained. "Sactalines are more accurately harvested from their places. They are found in some mountain ranges, but the seas of Merodia are the most plentiful."

"How are they harvested?" Savannah asked.

"All Sactalines are taken from a 'root', as it's called. Even as you look below you, you will notice large spires of Sactalines coming up out of the ground. As long as you don't take the entire thing down in one day, whatever you take will be replenished the next morning."

"Handy," Geoffrey commented. "No wonder you wanted controlling interests in the mines. It's an endless supply of money." Cyrus chuckled.

"Good idea, but that's not why I wanted this city. The further we explore, the more we find and the more new varieties we find. We've started to find some of them that are two colors or even three, or have a pattern. We don't even know the full potential or powers of these new Sactalines, but we have thousands of people working on them even as we speak. All together, the mines of Merodia run nearly one hundred miles in every direction."

"A hundred miles?" Geoffrey asked in disbelief. "That's amazing."

"No, what's amazing is what I'm about to show you next. Follow me." Cyrus led them through the glass hallway, which Geoffrey guessed was at least two miles long. Eventually it joined up to another large building like they had been in, Geoffrey was sure this one climbed all the way to the surface. Below them on the ocean floor, the sprawling buildings and halls bustled with activity.

They entered a large area with black walls and a white floor. The walls were lit with sactalines that shone teal in color. They lost sight of the mining facility for a moment or two until the entire wall next to them was made out of glass showing the truth depth and expanse of the mining operation.

They descended several more staircases until they were on the ground level on the ocean floor. They turned to the left where many doors stood. Cyrus approached and a different door appeared, seeming to reveal itself as though someone had pulled a curtain off it.

"Door number two," Cyrus announced. Cyrus opened the door and they stepped into a room filled with so much light that they could see nothing for several moments. They stood on a great balcony, overlooking a vast expanse. Countless rows and shelves lined the area below and on the shelves, crates and crates of Sactalines, of all colors and variety of colors, shining brightly.

"The store rooms of Merodia!" Cyrus announced. "There are six regular ones, and then there is this one. I have kept this one a secret for some time now."

"I'm speechless," Alexander managed. They walked down the stairs and slowly made their way through the rows. Geoffrey picked up a green and orange Sactaline and marveled at it.

"Why is this room separate?" Geoffrey asked after several minutes had passed.

"You, sir, have a cunning mind," Cyrus complimented. Geoffrey smiled to himself. "This is a room I had built especially for myself. As Minister I can make things disappear if I choose to. For some time now, I've been keeping nearly ninety percent of the Sactalines and storing them here for safe-keeping, until I could figure out what do with them."

Alexander and the others straightened, slowly coming around Cyrus.

"What are you going to do with them?" Alexander asked.

"I want to give them to the Kingdom," Cyrus announced. Geoffrey was taken aback, and he was sure his face had showed it to.

"Who's side are you on, exactly?" Geoffrey asked. He knew Alexander and Savannah were thinking the question, even if they hadn't spoken it yet.

"It would appear that I work for the Alliance, but there are other factors," Cyrus said. "I wish to align with the Kingdom." Now it was Alexander's turn to show surprise.

"You wish to become a Chrystarian?"

"No, I said I wish to align with the Kingdom. Hear me out on this. More and more every day, I'm learning or hearing about the horrors that Lucerine and the Alliance are causing. As a Hentarian Knight, I know this first hand, I've even been on a few missions that have left me with serious scars to my conscience. I have every reason to desert the Alliance and fully join the Kingdom."

"They why don't you?" Savannah asked.

"I have a few very good reasons why I won't do it right now, but I must keep these to myself. In the meantime, I don't see why I can't do my part in aiding the Kingdom. I would like to gift all of these and the research done on them to the Kingdom and do it for the remainder of this war."

"And no one would bat an eyelash if these went missing?"

"No one will miss them. If they don't go to the Kingdom, I will be forced to send them to the Alliance simply because I won't be able to store any more," Cyrus replied.

"I'm not sure I can give you an answer on this right away," Alexander said. "I feel like we should bring this up with Chrystar."

"Yes, I know, but if you will allow me. There is still one more door that I need to show you." The others followed him to a small door on the other side of the vast expanse. They entered into a dark shaft, which seemed to climb to the very top of the city. A single platform, made of a white rock floated down to them, a very strangely lit Sactaline was attached to the bottom of it. They climbed on the platform and took a seat as the platform began ascending at a great speed. The levels flew by until they reached the very top of the building.

They got off the platform and walked ahead to a small stair that led to a single door. Cyrus stopped when they reached the top of the stair. He smiled at them.

"Door number three!" He pushed the door open and strode through proudly. They were speechless as they looked down on a grand army, whose number they couldn't even guess.

"What in the—" Geoffrey started, though he trailed off.

"You said it!" Alexander exclaimed. "These troops do not belong to the Alliance do they?"

"No, they don't," Cyrus answered. He leaned casually against the railing as they continued to take everything in.

"They must be friendly with the Alliance, because they're right in the heart of Merodia," Savannah pointed out.

"Good logic, but wrong answer in this case," Cyrus said with a smile on his face.

"What are we missing?"

"These," Cyrus said, picking up a couple of blue and red Sactalines. Alexander took it. "They're a relatively new discovery. Among other things, it can make a large expanse of the land disappear. The Alliance has started using them to hide their intake camps. I decided I'd put them to good use as well. Only a handful of people know about this, all of which think the same as I do. The rest of the city sees an open space, which is for my own private use. No one is allowed to fly over, or set foot on this space. If it is violated, they may receive the penalty of death."

"I must say you are surprising me, Cyrus," Alexander said. "But in this case it is a welcomed surprise. But please tell us what are these people and what is an intake camp?"

"I don't know exactly, but it's another thing I needed to talk with you about," Cyrus said. Geoffrey studied him carefully, still unsure. "These people came from one of the six intake camps. All of them combined contain nearly a million people. The people you see below are from one of the intake camps. Along with a few faithful people helping me, I have been working to intercept and rescue as many as we can. They have sworn their allegiance to me and the Rebellion, with the intention of fighting against the Alliance."

"Rebellion?"

"Best name I could think of."

"So who are they? Prisoners of war?" Geoffrey asked.

Cyrus shrugged. "I have no idea. Every single person below has no records in any of the Alliance's archives. For all intents and purposes, they don't exist. It'll be up to the Kingdom to find and learn about these intake camps."

"Do you know anything else about these 'intake camps'?"

"Only that there's six of them. Also I'm not sure where all the people are coming from. Lucerine has laid waste to any city the Alliance has invaded and has left more people dead than alive. By all intelligence available to me, it doesn't add up. There's no way he should be producing nearly a million people and the resources needed for fighting the war, so swiftly."

"The Alliance is more fractured than I thought," Savannah replied. Cyrus nodded.

"Yes, but the facade is held together unnaturally well," Cyrus said. "I don't have the answer to anything, but I want to try and find out."

"I'm sure you realize you will be a marked man," Geoffrey said.

Cyrus nodded. "I know that, and am willing to accept whatever happens to me."

"Again I ask, why don't you just join the Kingdom now?" Alexander questioned.

"I have a few interests that are keeping my hands tied, and for that matter I think I need to play this role for the time being."

They all fell silent, thinking everything over carefully.

"If we say no to all of this, what is your plan with this army?" Geoffrey asked.

"I know the next three cities that are going to be attacked. I will send the Rebellion to fight the Alliance on all fronts."

"We need to talk to Chrystar and see what he thinks of all this," Alexander said.

"Yes of course," Cyrus agreed. "I'm willing to do anything in order to make this work."

"What are the cities to be attacked?"

"Heldar, Cordell, and the Triune Cliffs."

"Places currently not involved directly in the war," Savannah commented.

Cyrus nodded. "I'm sure you know that they have been helping the Kingdom secretly."

"Yes, we are aware. Savannah's sister-in-law is one of the underground contacts."

Several moments of silence passed between them.

"There is one more thing," Cyrus said. All three of them looked towards him knowingly. "Lucerine is obsessed with finding Roy and has nearly a thousand people searching for a doorway into his world. I don't know why he's so obsessed, but if he learns about Geoffrey, then Geoffrey will also be targeted."

"Comforting," Geoffrey commented.

"We need a place to talk and make some calls without fear of being found," Alexander said.

Cyrus nodded again. "You are my personal guests and shall stay in my home for as long as it is needed. Heldar is to be attacked in three days time, and if there is to be any trade or negotiations with the Kingdom I will make myself available at any time of the day."

"Very good," Alexander said, and they all agreed. The four of them began walking back the way they had come, and when they filed back through the store rooms, Alexander stared at a pile of grey Sactalines sitting on a shelf. He picked one up and held it in his hand. Cyrus came back to him, already sensing the question.

"What do these grey sactalines do?"

9

THE TWO WOMEN were carefully carried into the cabin and laid on cots that were placed in the spare bedroom. Within minutes a watch schedule had been created, with people keeping watch on both the cabin and the upstairs room, while the rest of them were allowed to go back to bed, and quickly fell asleep.

The upstairs room was still largely unchanged, but Roy and the others all thought they could vaguely see a faint outline of the doorway beginning to appear. Though over all, it was uncertain whether they were actually seeing it or if there mind was playing tricks on them.

Roy remained up, sitting in a chair and pondering everything. Evelyn had taken charge as soon as they had returned, turning the spare bedroom into the most efficient makeshift hospital that Roy had ever imagined. Jonathan remained up, helping in whatever way he could. Sylvia's injuries were extensive and time would tell what kind of scars would be left as a result.

Roy let his mind shift to the Hentarian Knight they had captured, still thrown off by the fact that it was a woman. It shouldn't have surprised him, as both the Alliance and the Kingdom had women at all levels in their ranks, but something about her had stood out to Roy.

Abby sat down in a matching chair and handed him a mug. He smiled as he took it from her. For a while they both sat in silence, each of them occupied in their own thoughts as they tried to process the events of the night.

"The day keeps getting more interesting," Roy commented finally.

"And it literally only started about two hours ago," Abby replied. They both smiled at the irony.

"Hopefully we can get some answers soon," Roy said.

Abby nodded. "Just be patient, my dear. We'll figure out what's going on. I am intrigued and slightly unnerved that there was so many Alliance soldiers in this world. I didn't think that was possible."

"I didn't either, but once Chrystar told me there were three ways between the worlds. Perhaps they've found one of the other ways," Roy suggested.

"What do you think their purpose in this world is?"

"At one time, Lucerine had a keen interest in me, perhaps he still does. Maybe Chrystar will have some better idea of what's going on." They both fell into silence for a moment, until Wiggs came running in from outside.

"Chrystar wants to speak with you," Wiggs said. He threw Roy a small green sactaline which Roy casually set on the arm of his chair.

"This is what I call some good timing," Roy said, smiling. "We were just saying we needed to get in contact with you."

"I thought you might be. How is everything going for you?" Chrystar asked. They brought him up to speed as quickly as they could.

"The thing we're unsure of is what to do now," Abby admitted. "First we thought we were waiting for the door to reappear, then we ended up caught in a firefight, and now we're sitting and waiting. Right now both our visitors are asleep. I'm not sure what else we can do until they wake up."

"I'm afraid you can't do anything, but keep your heads up. This may seem unplanned to you, and Lucerine no doubt thinks that he's pulled one over on me, but that couldn't be further from the truth. I completely anticipated this turns of events."

"That's comforting to know, but what's next?" Roy asked.

"I've just received some information from your brother's meeting," Chrystar said. "The person known as *'Trace'* who they were supposed to meet is in fact Abigail's brother, Cyrus. He has created an army of his own and wishes to fight against the Alliance."

"Has he switched sides?" Abby asked.

"Not officially, but I am to meet with him at Heldar the day after tomorrow."

"Is Heldar involved in the war? I thought they were neutral," Wiggs asked.

"He says the Alliance is going to attack there next. But aside from all that, there's a great amount of research going on in the realm of Sactalines, groundbreaking discoveries, and Cyrus has also turned all of that research over to the Kingdom."

"I am glad to know this, but I'm almost not sure I should believe it," Abby said.

"I understand, but remember even the hardest hearts can be turned with enough faith and persistence. Perhaps all of your kindness towards him has had an effect."

"What kindness?" Abby asked. "We've hardly spoken at all, since the war started."

"But you've all taken a silent vow, on both sides, not to kill each other," Chrystar let the fact hang for a moment. "I know other families within our ranks who have not been so fortunate."

"What other news do you have?" Roy asked after several moments of reflection.

"Currently, Gideon and I are buried in scrolls, books, and charts of the sort. There have been other off-worlder appearances over the centuries, a very small handful have been from places other than your cabin. We're trying our best to see if we can pinpoint a location of the entrances."

"Any luck so far?" Abby asked.

"Not particularly," Chrystar said. "However, just an hour ago, we did find a map with both worlds on it. I'm not sure how it matches up to the modern map that you might have, but it's a place to start."

"What should we do next?" Abby asked.

"Try your best to find the other two entrances. You have a Hentar Knight as a prisoner, so get whatever information out of her that you can. However, I caution you from using any force against her."

"Why's that?" Wiggs asked.

Roy smiled. "Because if we start off things the way they do, then we're no better then they are," Roy answered. "There's a time and a place for interrogation."

"Indeed," Chrystar agreed. "But I do not think you will need it this time. Sorry I can't talk more, but I must get busy with the Sactaline research Cyrus has sent us."

"Keep your eye out for any research pertaining to a grey Sactaline," Roy said. "We've found lots of them."

"Will do!" Chrystar exclaimed. "Until next time. Over and out." Roy gave the Sactaline to Wiggs who went back to his spot. Abby looked at him a light in her eyes, that he hadn't seen in a while. She raised her mug and he raised his in unison.

*   *   *   *

REBELLION

It was nearly midday until Roy and Abby were awoken from their slumber. Too tired to crawl to their bed they had curled up on the sofa. Jonathan stood to their side, a bottle of Mountain Dew in his hand.

"Good morning!" Jonathan greeted.

"What do you mean, good morning?" Roy asked.

"I mean, *good morning!*"

"Is it?"

"Is what?"

"Is this a good morning?" Roy asked.

"I thought so."

"You thought so?"

"Was I wrong?"

"Don't ask me. How would I know?" Roy said with a laugh. Abby smiled as they both stood up. "Indeed, it is a good morning, and it would've been a good morning whether you had wanted it or not!"

"I'm not sure what to make of that," Jonathan said. Both Roy and Abby laughed again.

"Off-worlder reference."

"Should've known," Jonathan replied. "What is this a reference to?"

"*The Hobbit.* That's how Gandalf the Grey first greets Bilbo Baggins," Roy replied.

Jonathan looked unamused. "See, this is what I don't understand about your world. When you say stuff like *Gandalf the 'Grey',* it is a most confusing thing. Is he grey? Is it the color of his beard? What is the 'grey'?"

"I'll let you figure it out," Roy said. Jonathan shot Abby a comical glance. "Anything new?"

"Yes, actually. Now that you're done peppering me with pointless questions, Sylvia and the other woman are awake."

"Have they said anything?" Abby asked.

"If they have, I wouldn't know about it, Evelyn has kept everyone out of the room since they woke up."

"Probably smart, we have one who's from our world and one who knows nothing about it," Abby said. "I'll see if us three can go in." Abby strode to the other side of the room and slipped through the door.

"So what happens in *The Hobbit?*" Jonathan asked.

"The main character, Bilbo, goes on an adventure with a bunch of dwarves to help them chase out a dragon from their old city," Roy replied.

Jonathan appeared deep in thought for a moment. "No wonder you caught on to our world so fast, if that's the kind of stuff you read about," Jonathan said.

Roy smiled. "A man without imagination is nothing."

"Fair enough," Jonathan said. Silence lingered for a moment. "What did the dragon do?"

"Took over their city and their treasure."

"So this Bilbo gets all the treasure at the end? Nice!"

"No, he only gets a ring."

"A ring?"

"Yes."

"Anything special about this ring?"

"Kind of." Jonathan looked at Roy hard.

"You can be very annoying, *Captain.*"

"Just read the book. It'll be easier."

Silence lingered for a moment before the door opened and Abby motioned to them. Roy and Jonathan eagerly made their way to the door and slipped inside. Evelyn and Abby blocked the way.

"Take it easy on them, okay?" Evelyn started. "The woman may be a Hentarian Knight, but she is also a young lady who has been through a lot, as of late."

REBELLION

"I understand," Roy said.

Abby slowly began walking over first to Sylvia who lay on her bed with numerous bandages and bruises. "Sylvia, I'm sorry we have to meet under these circumstances, but I am glad to see you alive."

"I thought I had died," Sylvia admitted. "What's going on?"

"We're not sure," Abby said. "But we were hoping you could tell us what happened?"

"What's going on, Roy?" Sylvia asked.

Roy hesitated, wondering how much he should say.

"What's going on, Jonathan?" Sylvia asked instead.

"When I bought this cabin," Roy explained so Jonathan wouldn't have to, "I discovered that the upstairs room was a portal to another world. I know that may be hard to—"

"Believe?" Sylvia asked. "I have a much easier time believing you after what I saw. Honestly, it would answer a lot of questions I had about you and Abby."

"I can only imagine," Roy replied. "What happened?"

"I had just gone to bed for the night, after driving Jonathan back here and the door on my house was broken down. Before I knew what was happening, I was being dragged out of bed and was being beaten and interrogated."

"What did they want?" Jonathan asked.

"They wanted to know where I had taken you," Sylvia answered. "No matter what they did to me, something inside of me couldn't bring myself to give them that information. I was tortured for what seemed like an eternity. Finally, by some miracle the attack was called off and they left me."

"That's unusual for Alliance to do that," Abby said. "What happened to make them leave?"

82

"I'm not sure," Sylvia admitted.

"I called off the attack," the other woman said. Her voice was rich and gentle, but filled with remorse. Everyone seemed to ponder over her choice of words as they waited for her to speak again. The woman stared into the space in front of her and didn't move. Her leg was wrapped up tightly, having been injured, but not so bad as she wouldn't be able to walk if she wanted to.

"You called off the attack?" Abby asked again.

"Yes," the woman answered, more confidently this time. "I called it off because I knew she wasn't going to tell us what I wanted to know. I also suspected that she wasn't going to hold out much longer."

"You thought she would die?" Jonathan asked.

"I knew she would. The Hentar don't waste time. We are trained to read a mark quickly and decisively. What we say, goes. If we know that we are not going to get what we want from a subject, according to the governing laws the Hentarian in charge, in this case me, would be required to kill the person."

"Why did you leave her for dead instead of kill her as your laws dictate?" Evelyn asked.

The woman stared into the distance for a moment. "Because I couldn't bring myself to kill another innocent person. I knew she would live if we stopped, so I told the others she was as good as dead and left," the woman said. "Curse me for being so weak!"

"What some say is weakness is sometimes strength," Sylvia chimed in.

Roy thought the woman's features softened at the words.

"Why would it be counted as strength?" she asked.

"Courage is not knowing when to take a life, but when to spare one," Roy explained.

The woman looked down at her hands as if she was ashamed. "That's not what Hentar are taught."

"Maybe it's time to listen to some new teaching?" Evelyn suggested. The woman remained silent, looking off into the distance. If she was pondering some great mystery none of them knew what it was. "What's your name, sweetheart?"

"Christina Munithal," the woman replied. Roy studied the woman closely as she said the name two more times, under her breath, as if she wasn't used to hearing her own name.

"It's a pleasure to meet you," Abby said.

"It's a pleasure to meet you as well," Christina replied. "You're Abigail and Roy Van Doren?"

"Yes," Roy replied. "How'd you know that?"

"I was looking for you," Christina said. They were all taken aback and left speechless for a moment or two.

"Looking for me?" Roy asked.

Christina nodded.

"How do you mean that?"

"Capturing you is all Lucerine talks about."

"Since you seem to be so forthcoming, why is Lucerine so interested in Roy, aside from him being an off-worlder?" Evelyn asked.

"He wishes to see Roy and any who are with him brought to Bruden, tortured and interrogated until he gives up the location of the doorway into the other world...or the one we're currently in."

"What do they hope to accomplish with all of the theatrics?" Roy asked.

"The Alliance, despite the face they put on, is not doing as well as everyone is led to believe. The Kingdom has done far better at fighting back and turning people's perception than Lucerine wants to admit. That being the case, Lucerine's had the idea to find a way into this world, and to collect resources and people to fight in his armies. He was quite obsessed with the fact that there are three entrances that we need to find."

"Apparently he's found one of them, or else you wouldn't be here," Roy replied.

"Yes, he has found it, but there's a twist. I have no memory of it," Christina told them. "I know it sounds like just a line, but The Alliance has come across some new Sactalines with strange powers. I think they have one that blocks whatever is happening from your memory."

"Do you know this ability for certain?" Abby asked.

"The Hentar have used these for years on our security teams, mostly. Left the people with less scars. They've never before worked on Hentarian Knights."

"And you expect us to believe you now?" Jonathan asked.

Christina looked away for a moment.

"What I say it true, whether you believe it or not. These new Sactalines have weird powers. I may have come into this world knowing what we were going to do, but the last thing I *remember* is laying down to sleep in Bruden."

They all pondered the possibilities for a moment.

"If what you say is true, how were you supposed to know where to take the people?" Roy asked.

"I don't know where they went. Only the pilots were told, and that's besides the point. If they had any of these Sactalines on them, then they would not remember anything when it's all said and done."

"I'm not sure what to make of all this," Sylvia said. Jonathan gently put a hand on her shoulder.

"Why are you in this world?" Roy asked. "You said you were looking for us. Why?"

"So I can save you," Christina answered. "You are not as safe as you think you are. Lucerine is actively searching for you. He needs all three entrances for something. But whatever it is, I don't want him to get it."

"Do you know what this does?" Roy asked, pulling a grey sactaline out of his pocket.

Christina instantly shuddered. "Those were in town, weren't they?"

Roy nodded.

"How many do you have?"

"All of them we could find."

Christina's face washed white with fear. "We don't have much time!"

With surprising speed, Christina hobbled from her spot towards the door. Roy and Jonathan both instinctively blocked it, preventing a hysterical Christina from escaping the bedroom. Evelyn and Abby grabbed her and gently moved her away from the door, convincing her to take a seat on the edge of the bed. Slowly Roy relaxed as Christina began calming down.

"What's wrong?" Evelyn asked.

Christina hesitated. "Those grey sactalines are tracking sactalines. Certain people can feel their presence and detect where they are hidden. It's how we know which town to strike. The more you have, the stronger the signal."

"So if they know the sactalines are here?" Roy asked.

Christina nodded. "It won't be long before they're here."

"Puts us in a tight spot," Jonathan said.

"Where are we going to go?" Sylvia asked.

Roy thought for a moment. "I'm not sure," he admitted. "Obviously Sylvia's got some cracked ribs and injuries that are going to make it hard to move anywhere fast. Even Christina's going to have a hard time on that leg."

"If I have to cut my leg off, I will. I can't let them capture me!" Christina cried.

"Why not?" Jonathan asked. "Seems like it might be a good trade—you for our safety."

In an instant Christina's face was filled with fear and for the first time Roy believed everything she had told them.

"Please, I beg of you no!" Christina pleaded. "I-I-I-I have to get home—but I can't go with them!" She burst into tears. Abby and Evelyn both embraced her. Finally, Christina composed herself. "I've been trying to be free of them for years, and I've never had a chance like this! I need to get home on my own. Please! I'll help you. We need to leave this cabin and find one of the other doors into our world."

All eyes turned to Roy, who was deep in thought. He looked into Christina's eyes, able to confirm all that he needed to know. She *was* telling the truth. What her whole story was he couldn't say, but with each second that passed, he knew that the past didn't matter.

"My team and I are going to step outside and talk for a minute, and then we'll be back." Jonathan stayed in the room while Evelyn and Abby followed Roy out. The house was still mostly silent, with a few team members lingering. The rest were on patrols of some kind.

"What do you want to do, Roy?" Evelyn asked.

"Do you think she's telling the truth?" Roy asked.

Abby and Evelyn both nodded.

"She could be acting, but she seems a little too desperate for that," Evelyn replied. "Besides, she would have nothing to gain by acting. So far in my conversations with her, she hasn't changed any stories or facts. I believe her."

"She passes my test," Abby said. "The true test, though, will be whether we are attacked or not."

"Can we get Chrystar or Gideon on the Sactaline by any chance?" Roy asked. Evelyn nodded and slipped away for a minute or two. Abby and Roy made their way to the upstairs room, surprised to find that they could see the door, plain as day.

"Showed up about a minute ago," Wiggs said, from his chair in the middle of the room. "I was just about to come get you." Roy smiled and strode to the door, grasping the handle and pulling. To everyone's surprise the door didn't budge.

"Can't get it open," Roy said after several more tries.

"How many oddities can we have in one day?" Abby asked.

"One more, apparently," Wiggs replied. "Then again I suppose it *is* a new day so we're all good."

They smiled at the comment. Evelyn came into the room holding a green sactaline.

"I've got Gideon for you," Evelyn said, noticing the door.

"Gideon!" Roy greeted. "Good to hear from you."

"You as well!" Gideon said. "I have truly never been surrounded by so many charts, parchments, and scrolls in my life. I'm think I'm starting to loose my mind."

"Is that because of the research or due to taking care of the girls all the time?" Evelyn teased. They could imagine Gideon smiling on the other end.

"We're doing good on that front, though Henley and Bristol were trying really hard to tell me how to do their hair and I was lost. I am thankful that Ember's old enough to do hair and all that girly stuff that I know nothing about, otherwise I'd loose my mind." They all chuckled.

"I think you lost that many years ago, hon," Evelyn said.

"Ah, yes, the day I fell in love with you!" Gideon replied, and they all chuckled.

"We've got weird stuff going on here," Roy explained. "The door has reappeared in my upstairs room, but it won't open. Not even a wiggle. We also captured a Hentarian Knight, only to our surprise, she fully wants to help us. And supposedly grey Sactalines are tracking Sactalines and may bring the Alliance right to our doorstep."

"You sure aren't bored, are you?" Gideon asked teasingly.

"We wish we were," Abby said.

"Okay, so the door thing is strange. I can tentatively confirm the fact about the grey Sactaline. The Kingdom received a large donation of Sactalines and research, and I think I remember reading that." There was a pause. "Did you really capture a Hentarian Knight?"

"Yeah, she claims that the Alliance is searching for all three doors into this world. She doesn't know why," Abby answered.

"Okay..."

"She says we need to leave this cabin before it's discovered and find the second doorway. Has your research turned up anything?"

"Yes, and I will say I've had just about enough of this researching doors business."

"Do tell?" Evelyn asked.

"I've been buried in the library looking over charts and maps that are way older than I might have imagined. It is not clear who or how these doors came to be in the first place. It just doesn't make sense."

"Sure about that?" Roy asked teasingly.

"Okay, so it makes sense, but it doesn't make it any easier for my human brain to understand."

"Ah, but if we understood everything about our creator, then there wouldn't be any creator would there?"

"True enough, true enough," Gideon said. "If we understood everything about him than it would be proof that we created him. Which is of course, impossible. I always knew you were my brightest student!"

"Now about the doors?" Evelyn asked.

"Ah, yes! Sorry, dear. I've managed to compare about ten maps that were

89

drawn of the your mountains, and where off-worlders thought they were, and I believe I have a location for you."

"That's great!" they all exclaimed.

"It looks to be about thirty miles north of your cabin, as the Griffin flies."

"To bad we didn't have a Griffin," Abby said.

"To bad we don't have Geoffrey here," Roy reflected. There was a indistinct chatter and papers shuffling on the other end.

"Okay, it's official, the grey Sactalines are tracking Sactalines!" Gideon announced. "I would recommend getting out of there as soon as possible, and heading towards the coordinates I'll give you."

"Sounds good," Roy replied. "I'll have Jonathan come up in a minute."

"One more thing, Roy!"

"I'm listening."

"If they are convinced they need all three doors, that means they are looking for *all* three doors. If they come to your cabin—"

"They'll find a door that doesn't work."

"Doesn't work right now," Gideon pointed out. "We don't know what the secrets of these doors are. I'm not there, so I can't make any decision for you, but you can't just let them *have* the house."

Roy and Abby exchanged glances, knowing what was being suggested.

"We understand," Abby replied.

"I'm sure you do."

Roy and Abby excused themselves and sent for Jonathan, who came and got the coordinates of the supposed second door from Gideon. Meanwhile, they went downstairs and sat silent for several minutes as they processed the new information.

"Never thought we'd have to leave this place," Abby said.

"Maybe we'll get to come back and rebuild when the war's over," Roy replied. They fell silent again.

"If they're going to destroy this place," Abby announced, "they shouldn't get it without a fight!"

10

THOUGH STILL SKEPTICAL of Cyrus's motives, Geoffrey found himself more and more relaxed around him. A day and a half had passed, and now the four of them were mere minutes away from leaving to meet Chrystar at Heldar.

"I sure hope your conversation with Chrystar goes well," Alexander said to Cyrus. "I'm looking forward to fighting alongside you, even if it doesn't look like we're fighting together."

"Indeed. I'm sorry about the way things played out the last time, but please understand, there are reasons I did what I did," Cyrus said.

"We understand," Savannah replied. "I'm still curious to know your motive behind all of it."

"I'm sorry I was blind to it for so long. Though I wasn't blind, I was trapped. And that perhaps is the worst of all."

"And how are you now?" Geoffrey asked.

"Still trapped, but at least there's a light at the end of the tunnel." They finished eating their meal until there came a group of soldiers, led by an important looking person, coming across the room towards them.

"Our escorts," Cyrus said. They rose and followed Cyrus's lead as they were led away from their rooms and then joined by several more groups of soldiers. Geoffrey began to feel uncomfortable as the number became greater and greater. Despite their disguises, he felt insecure.

They walked for several minutes until they reached the main landing bay where they had landed their own Dreygar a day and a half ago. Everything that Cyrus had requested was ready and waiting for them.

"Soldiers up high," Geoffrey whispered. Alexander looked up to the next level balcony which they hadn't noticed when they had arrived. Nearly a hundred soldiers lined the railing.

"Cyrus!" Alexander exclaimed in as much of a whisper as possible.

"I see it," Cyrus replied. "Follow my lead." They strode confidently up to what Geoffrey assumed was a customary line of dignitaries that were here to see off their Minister.

"We wish you all the best in your trip my Minister," the first person said.

"Thank you very much. I will only be gone for a day, make sure the city does not fall apart while I'm gone."

"The Alliance is in control. How could it fall apart?" the person said. They both laughed.

"Indeed, as long as those cursed Chrystarians don't touch it, we'll all live happily ever after."

"Well said," the person agreed. Their blood ran cold as the voice this time was different. It was deeper and more gravely. In an instant, the person changed form, revealing a figure in a long black cloak. His hair was long and his eyes were filled with vengeance. His face, though it seemed as if though it should look young, looked old and worn down.

"Who?" Geoffrey whispered to Savannah.

"Lucerine, the leader of the Alliance," she whispered almost before he had asked the question. The onlookers gasped and bowed to their leader. Lucerine now stood tall and proud.

"You speak good words, Cyrus. I'll give you that," Lucerine said. Everyone stood back to their feet. "But lately I've questioned some motives of yours, and I figured I had to see the place for myself. You really have done a lot with this city, from what I hear."

"It would be an honor to have you as a guest, my lord," Cyrus said. "However, I am on my way out of town on business."

"And this business is more important than your lord and king?" Lucerine asked.

"Of course not! I was merely saying that direct action is the best offensive, and forgive me, but I was not expecting you. Name what you wish and I will grant it."

"I've come to inquire about those new Sactalines you told me about. I want to get them into the possession of the Alliance in a little under a week."

"We were putting the final preparations on the shipping as we speak," Cyrus explained.

"Of course," Lucerine said. "I've come this far. I wouldn't mind seeing the Sactalines for myself! You've peaked my interest with your recent communications."

"Certainly. Please allow me to make you comfortable while I gather my thoughts, and then I'll meet with you."

"Of course," Lucerine said. Fully satisfied, he was joined by some men of Cyrus's and led away into a hall somewhere on the left side. As soon as Lucerine was out of sight, the foursome turned and headed back through the soldiers and into the hall they had just come out of.

"This is getting a little too close for comfort!" Alexander exclaimed. Cyrus walked quickly as they ducked into an open meeting room and closed the door.

"To close for me, too!" Cyrus said. "I had all those shipped to the Kingdom yesterday. I have nothing to show him!"

"What are you going to do?" Geoffrey asked.

"I'm not sure. This is not how it was supposed to go!" Cyrus said.

"Maybe it's not the way you planned it, but someone had this planned." Geoffrey replied.

The statement left Cyrus speechless. "You're saying that everything I've done is doomed to failure? I'm trying to help the good guys for a change, and this is what happens to me!"

"You had a good plan," Alexander said. "But perhaps there is something greater at work. You reached out to the Kingdom, and out of all the people who could have met you here it was us, your family. Perhaps we were brought here for such a time as this, even if it seems hopeless."

"What are we going to do?"

"You said you were ready to put yourself on the map. Send your Rebellion army into action. Maybe it's time to take a stand," Savannah suggested. Geoffrey nodded his approval, and for a moment all time seemed to stop.

"So, throw away the double agent and just join the Kingdom?" Cyrus asked. "I don't know if the Kingdom will even accept me."

"It's clear you haven't met Chrystar yet, but I think it's safe to say that he can be far more reasonable than you might think," Alexander encouraged.

"I haven't known him that long, and I understand that," Geoffrey added. "What will it be, Cyrus? Take a stand or take a backseat? I'm pretty sure there is no middle road here."

"It's the right thing to do," Cyrus said, mostly to himself. "Why does the right thing have to be so hard?"

"Because Chrystar asks for the heart, not the head. It's hard to give up your heart to anyone, let alone, risking it all and having faith that there's something greater at work," Savannah said.

Cyrus seemed to consider her words. "I can't promise we'll come out of this alive," he said.

"We didn't ask for that," Alexander said. "But we're here to fight what is evil in this world, first and foremost the Alliance." The four of them smiled and came closer, each of them formulating a plan in their minds.

"We have ten minutes to figure out how to get out of this mess," Cyrus said. "And if you'll trust me, I think I know how we can." Geoffrey scanned the room and hastily poured four glasses of some beverage. He handed one to each of them.

"To family?" Geoffrey asked.

Cyrus smiled and raised his glass. "To family!"

*   *   *   *

Alexander was amazed at how quickly everything had been organized. Ten minutes after Cyrus had made his decision, he and Savannah stood at the front of a large army. The people the army consisted of were clearly not skilled or trained warriors, but regardless, they strapped their swords on and held their bows with the same attitude of selfless determination.

A few seconds dragged on as they waited to attack the unsuspecting Alliance army. Geoffrey and Cyrus had already left, having taken a secret entrance out of the city, figuring that out of the four of them, they were the most sought after.

"We await your orders, General," one of the commanders said though the new Sactalines they had been given.

"On our mark, form up behind us," Alexander said. "Urir will take his group to the east and secure the perimeter, Traceadox will take his to the west and do the same. Yula will follow behind us and head for the city center. Strike any and all staging areas and large groups of Dreygars and Alliance troops you see, including weapons. We're going for a big bang here. If we're lucky, we'll free the city and live to tell the tale. Remember, no targeting of civilians!" Alexander said.

"Yes, General," came the reply from all three.

"Air units, do your best to take out any defenses you see before they become threats, and drop off your troops at the landing sites told to you previously," Savannah reminded.

"We're in the shaft," Geoffrey's voice came through the Sactaline. "See you on the flip side!"

"Commanders, mark our positions and don't pass the Sactalines until we do," Alexander exclaimed. All at once the Dreygars they rode upon, pushed up into the air. Savannah and Alexander marveled at the speed of these particular Dreygars, as opposed to the previous Dreygar they had ridden. The others had seemed slow and labored, but these ones seemed to effortlessly glide into the air.

Everyone else behind them took flight, breaking into their three separate groups as planned. All at once they turned and flew directly at the Sactalines that were shielding them from being seen.

They broke free of the screen and immediately began firing upon their targets, making sure to keep any civilian structure from being intentionally struck by stray arrows.

The Alliance troops scrambled around, unsure of what was happening, as it appeared to them that they were being attacked by themselves. Alexander took aim at a supply bridge that traversed the city. A moment later it was lit up in fire and flames, and chunks of stone cascaded down to the platform far below.

They flew at amazing speeds through the maze of tall buildings. Alexander watched Savannah, amazed and impressed as she seemed to effortlessly maneuver through oncoming arrows and debris.

It was several minutes until the armor on the Dreygar lit up with a fiery blast.

"That was quicker I expected," Savannah said, mostly to herself. Then she spoke into her Sactaline. "Looks like someone's starting to figure out what we're doing. Keep pressing towards your targets, but be ready for anything they try!"

Even as she finished speaking, a large building in front of them was pelted with more arrows than Alexander could count. The entire horizon in front of them was filled with flames and when the flames and smoke dispersed, they could see what had happened.

The building in front of them began to lean as the entire base of it had been destroyed by the arrows. Savannah and Alexander held on and urged the Dreygar faster, knowing there was no time to pull up now. Savannah pushed them into a dive, racing against time and the building that was now plunging towards them.

They passed under the falling building and came through on the other side. The building crashed into the other buildings beneath it, crushing them into oblivion. Several of their Dreygars were taken out as the building crashed.

Alexander instructed the men where to aim and they returned fire to those who had fired upon them. All across the city, large explosions lit up the sky as the other teams illuminated their targets. The time and distance they traveled seemed to fade in their minds, making it easier to keep motivated about their task.

They turned hard to the left seeing their target straight ahead. The men aboard split up, with half of them drawing their swords and the other half remaining on the bows.

They flew over the city and then emerged to a large open expanse.

Alexander and Savannah looked down in shock and horror as the entire space was empty.

"What's going on?" Alexander said. "This is supposed to be the main staging area."

"Unless we were told wrong," Savannah said. However, as she finished speaking, hundreds of Tantine bolts flew through the air, all of them coming in their direction. Everyone drew their swords and deflected as many arrows as they could, while the armor on the Dreygar lit up all the rest. For a moment, Alexander could see nothing. The fire wrapped around them, but didn't hurt them.

When it cleared they were greeted by a grim reality. The armor on the Dreygar was spent and they had no extra. Ahead of them, more arrows came flying through the air, these ones aimed lower, directly at the Dreygar that Alexander and Savannah were on. The arrows struck the Dreygar, who instantly went limp and began falling out of the sky.

"Stay away from final staging area!" Savannah yelled through the Sactaline. "Stay away from the staging area! Hit your targets and get to the rendezvous point!"

The Dreygar continued to plummet out of the sky and then crashed onto the ground. Everyone frantically jumped to their feet and drew their swords. A moment later they were met by arrows and a battle cry as large masses of Alliance troops, led by at least fifty Hentarian Knights rushed to surround them.

In an instant they were swept up into a battle, that had everyone involved blocking both arrows and the swords of their enemies. Despite the odds, Savannah and Alexander stood strong with their men, who had gathered around.

Explosions still echoed throughout the city, but the longer the fight went on, the more Alexander knew they would never walk away from this one.

REBELLION

More Alliance troops landed and replenished any that they had taken down, and now even a few of their own had fallen.

The Hentarian Knights viciously attacked, leaping and swinging wherever they pleased. Alexander and Savannah both blocked and took down several of them, but soon found themselves pressed up against a brick wall.

Everyone, even the Hentarian Knights stopped their attacking, seeming pleased with themselves, and to Alexander it looked like they were waiting for something. He quickly glanced over to Savannah, who was noting the same thing. A quick nod from their remaining troops told them that everyone was thinking the same thing.

They all carefully watched Savannah whose fingers were flirting with the hilt of her sword. A Dreygar larger than all the rest appeared in the distance and no one had to ask who was on it, because it became evident. Every soldier in the clearing bowed to the ground as Lucerine descended.

Seizing the opportunity, Savannah drew her sword and brandished it. The others did the same and rushed towards her, touching the blades together. A terrible flash of light consumed the blades as lighting tore through the air and struck all the Alliance soldiers instantly.

The soldiers fell to the ground and the approaching Dreygar hesitated as if reconsidering. Joy filled them all, but then vanished just as quickly as it had come. Their swords became like lead and their hands were loosed from the hilts. They were pulled back to the wall and found themselves in chains. The Dreygar approached and landed, a black cloaked figure dismounted.

"As promised, my lord," Cyrus said from the side. He strode in confidently.

Alexander both looked at him, confusion and anger running through him.

"I've caught the leaders of the Rebellion army."

"Good work, Cyrus," Lucerine complimented.

"I'm only sorry that so many Alliance troops were killed in the process." Lucerine scoffed. "Though they are mere pawns in a game of chess—valuable, but easily replaced if they are spent. But, you said there would be a third. Where did he go?"

"The third one got away, my lord, but don't worry. He will be butchered before nightfall."

"Make it so, and there may be another promotion in it for you," Lucerine said. Cyrus nodded in agreement. "Get these ready for transport and then meet me inside." Lucerine left without speaking another word, soon he was in the building.

"Sorry, guys, but this is really going to make sense later."

"You're taking us prisoner! What kind of sense does that make?" Alexander asked.

Cyrus looked at him with a sinister smile. "No matter what happens, I need you to remember this...it was Geoffrey's idea."

11

"THEY'RE PROBABLY FIVE minutes out," Victor told them through the Sactaline. "Why they're coming on foot, though, I can't guess."

"Maybe they wanted the exercise," Jonathan said. A couple chuckles from everyone brought a smile to Roy's face.

"More likely, they're off snatching other helpless citizens," Christina said. Her voice hinted at sorrow, though she had kept most of it from the notice of the others. Despite their best efforts to convince Christina to leave the cabin early with many of the others, she had refused. "I feel hopeless just waiting."

"So do I," Roy admitted. "But all for a good cause. We've prepared all that we can. Now all we have to do is take a stand."

"What are we standing against?" Christina asked.

"Against people not having the free choice that God gave them," Abby said. "To not have a choice is not love at all, God gave us the choice to follow him. But it's up to us to choose it."

"I don't quite understand what you're talking about," Christina admitted. "But I know what you're talking about. I've spent years trapped in a life I couldn't escape, only to feel like all hope had been drained from me, until I was nothing but a worthless piece of trash."

"You need to get out more," Jonathan teased.

To their surprise Christina laughed and smiled at the remark. "I'm

102

working on it."

They fell silent, looking and waiting for something to happen. Sylvia and most of the others had already left, beginning their travels to the coordinates that Gideon had given them. The team that remained was scattered around the property, ready to close in on the Alliance troops which were steadily growing closer.

The five minutes went quickly, and finally a single tap of a fingernail came through the Sactaline, signaling that Victor could see the soldiers. They readied their weapons and waited.

Roy glanced in Christina's direction. "You sure you want to do this?"

"I need to do this."

"There will be only a small window to pull it off and with your injuries, I'm not sure how it'll go."

"I know," Christina said. "I helped to create this mess. I want to be the one to finish it."

"Very well," Roy replied, speaking to his Sactaline. "The plan stays the same. Get them in the house."

A minute later, the first soldier could be faintly seen stepping into the clearing.

"Arrows ready!" Roy exclaimed in a whisper. They all raised their crossbows, reading their shots from their spot on the backside of the property. The front of the house faced away from them.

Roy fired the first arrow, illuminating the dark night as it streaked across the property. It found its target, letting off a tremendous flash as it struck the armor of the soldier. Everyone else let their arrows fly, cries and curses poured from the soldiers they had fired on.

Return arrows came thundering in their direction, though many of them missed their marks and flew wide of their targets. Many struck the trees around them, forcing some of Roy's team to quickly move out of the way.

REBELLION

The soldiers below scattered this way and that, trying to figure out what was going on as the rest of the soldiers came running into the clearing.

Roy let a smile spread across his face as he watched the soldiers, one by one, begin making their way into the cabin.

His rejoicing was short lived as arrows came at his team from the side, catching all of them unaware. The arrows struck their armor and they were forced to turn towards the source of the attack. A large group of soldiers came through the trees, rushing towards them. Roy was the first to stand and draw his sword. Another cry came up from the other side of them.

"Time to get out of here!" Jonathan exclaimed. Roy turned to Abby and Christina, his heart racing when neither of them were anywhere to be found.

A moment later they were engaged in a fiery exchange of arrows and swords as they did their best to take as many down as they could. The group of soldiers who had at first taken refuge in the house, now came out and closed in on them.

"Teams on the front of the house hold your fire. Everyone else lay down your arms. They win this round." Roy dropped his sword and put his hands up and everyone else with him did the same. They were overcome by the soldiers who at once had stopped using weapons.

*   *   *   *

Roy's face felt numb from being struck so many times. He was on his knees in the middle of his now ransacked cabin. The Alliance soldiers had torn it apart, claiming to be searching for anything of importance. The other six of his team that were still with him, were bound and tied to the wall nearest the staircase. In total, fifty soldiers had shown up. Roy was held by several soldiers on either side of him.

"How do we get the door open?" the man in charge asked again. He was slightly greying and altogether had a horrible complexion.

"I don't know," Roy answered, truthfully. He received another punch to the face as a response.

"How is it that the great Roy Van Doren, does not know about this aspect of a cabin that you own?!" the man yelled.

"If I knew how to get the door open then I would've done it by now, as opposed to having this lovely conversation." He received another round of beatings.

"You clearly are not familiar with the ways of the Hentar. We have ways to handle people who do not answer the questions that we ask. Let's introduce a new tactic." He motioned for someone to come forward. They handed him a sheathed dagger. "No ordinary dagger. This is a weapon from an ancient time."

He pulled the blade out and revealed that it glowed a fiery red.

"Looks hot, but it is cool to the touch if you are a Hentarian, which you aren't. Each second it touches your skin, a searing pain penetrates your mind. A few minutes of this will leave even the strongest person quivering in fear." He paused. "They are much more forthcoming after this. I don't think you'll be any different, because I'm going to use it on one of your friends."

He motioned and Jonathan was dragged from his spot and forced to the ground in front of Roy. The man held the dagger at the ready.

"The nice thing about this weapon is I don't have to physically cut him for it to work." The man seemed to beam and he brandished the weapon, as if showing off a great prize. In an instant he touched the blade to Jonathan's neck. The house was immediately filled with Jonathan's cries as the weapon torched him. "Perhaps you'd like to know what he's feeling right about now." Another dagger was produced and instantly touched to Roy's skin.

His mind burned with fire and every nerve in his body throbbed with pain as though he was being electrocuted endlessly. For several more minutes he and Jonathan endured until finally, without warning the weapons were pulled away and their thoughts returned. They were beaten until finally their captor stood over them once again.

"Not so pleasant, is it?" the man taunted. "Will you tell me what I want to know?"

"I will not," Roy said. Jonathan nodded his agreement.

"Then we'll do another round. I would warn that the longer you're in contact with this weapon, the worse the affects. With it I can turn you into a groveling mad man, a crazed lunatic, or I can do it for so long that it will kill you." He didn't wait for a response as they were once again thrust into a world of pain and misery.

The torture continued for several minutes until a loud sound could be heard. They found their hope flooding back to them like a tidal wave. What the sound was, none of them knew, for certain, but it sounded like a low rumble that was steadily gaining momentum.

The weapons were pulled from their necks and their senses returned to them, immediately allowing them to figure out what was going on. Roy and Jonathan both stood and jumped to the left. It was just in time as the back end of Roy's truck came crashing through the front porch and wall of the cabin.

Jonathan and Roy immediately scrambled to their feet and everyone other member of their team took advantage of the stunned soldiers. Abby

106

grinned widely in the front seat of the truck.

"I know I've never driven this truck before, but that was a lot of fun!"

"Get in, everyone!" Roy called. Everyone scrambled to get in the back. "Although I'm not sure if we're better off here or with Abby driving!" They laughed and held their breath as Abby put the truck in gear and sent the truck rocketing forward. They reached the forest edge and she slammed on the brakes.

"What's going on?" Jonathan asked.

"Favor for a friend," Abby said, getting out of the truck. They turned to see the house with a gaping hole in the side of it and all the Alliance troops standing there shell shocked.

In the faint light they could see one person striding up to the cabin with difficulty. And to their surprise, that person was dressed in the armor of a Chrystarian.

"Trintin!" Christina called out.

The person who had been interrogating them looked out in surprise.

"Well, well, well, how the mighty have fallen?" Trintin taunted. "If it isn't the one we've all been measured to, all our lives."

"Cut the flattery. Trintin. It isn't going to save you!"

"Oh, and who's going to kill me? You?" Several of the others chuckled. "What have I ever done to you?"

"You killed Allison. That's all the reason *I* need," Christina replied.

"Your sister was a weak, spineless piece of flesh. Call it a mercy killing."

"She's still my sister."

"Yeah, and what of it? I had orders, and I followed them. Got myself a nice promotion in the process," Trintin called back. "You could say that your sister's death was not in vain. I certainly benefited from it." The other Alliance soldiers inside the cabin laughed and some cheered.

What Christina's face expressed Roy couldn't guess, as her back was turned to them. She pulled a crossbow and leveled it at him.

"So you've turned to *their* side, have you?"

"I'm certainly not on yours," Christina replied.

"Guess it makes sense why you killed your apprentice at the start of the war. You were going soft, and he was going to kill you!" Trintin jeered. "I'm not afraid of you."

"You don't think I'm going to kill you?" Christina asked.

"If you had it in you, you would've done it by now. Besides, I stand before you unarmed. Shooting an unarmed person? Sounds like that's something that goes against the *Chrystarian* code."

"You know what?" Christina asked. "You're right. But, let's get one thing straight..." She fired a bolt from the cross-bow. It struck him in the knee between the armor. He staggered to his knees, the other soldiers with him were too surprised to do anything.

Christina looked at Trintin for a moment. "I may be on my road to redemption...but I'm not a saint, yet! This is for Allison!" Before anyone could speak, she fired another arrow, which struck Trintin in the head. "And this is for everything else!" she stepped back and fired twenty arrows into the cabin, intentionally aiming for the floor or the walls.

The clearing was filled with fire and smoke as the cabin was blown to bits, debris flying high into the sky.

Christina turned from the burning rubble and came to join them by the truck. "I know it might be bad to say, but that felt really good!"

The others smiled weakly. "I'm sure Chrystar will understand," Evelyn said. "I think you've proved where you heart doesn't lie."

Christina smiled. "What now, Captain?" she asked.

"We start moving. We'll pick the others up if we see them. Otherwise, we get to the coordinates Gideon gave us and see what's there. We've got thirty miles as the Griffin flies, and time is ticking."

A couple of the crew helped Christina into the cab of the truck.

Roy turned to Abby. "If it's okay, I think I'll drive now."

"Are you kidding?" Abby asked with a wink and a smile. "This is fun!"

12

GEOFFREY FOLLOWED BEHIND CYRUS. The hall in front of them was empty. The building shook and rattled, and the sounds of war could still be heard all throughout Merodia. Cyrus had rightly guessed that with the Alliance busy fighting the Rebellion army, there would be few guards in this part of the city. So far they hadn't seen anyone.

A few minutes later they emerged from the deserted hallway and stood in a large opening that was about five hundred feet to the other side. It was a similar shaft to the one that they had been in earlier, however this one was far older. Geoffrey knew it wouldn't be near as relaxing.

"Here we go!" Cyrus exclaimed. With surprising ease he lowered himself over the side and grasped the ledge with his fingers. Slowly he began making his way down the side of the shaft, using cracks in the side of the shaft to walk his way down like a ladder.

Geoffrey held his breath and willed himself to follow in Cyrus's footsteps as they began climbing down at what seemed like a very slow pace.

"Who's idea was this?" Geoffrey asked.

"Yours," Cyrus answered.

"I think I'm regretting this decision."

"Oh! I think Geoffrey is a little scared," Cyrus said.

"Yes. Yes, Geoffrey is a little scared."

Cyrus smiled. "So am I."

They climbed in silence, descending past level after level with no sign that they were any closer to their destination. The air became cooler and more damp and the sounds of the war outside became more distant and muffled, although they could still feel the building shaking on occasion.

Finally they reached their destination and crawled into the opening, which revealed a long dark tunnel. There was minimal light, with only a few Sactalines placed every so often.

"Are you sure they were put down here?" Geoffrey asked.

"No, but it's where I ordered them to be put, so it should have been done," Cyrus answered. They walked a while more through the dark, until they finally came to another long hall which was lined on either side with prison cells. They looked in the first few cells, finding nothing. Five minutes later they came to a cell with two shadows in it. They came closer, seeing Alexander and Savannah lying together on the cold hard floor.

Geoffrey smiled widely. "Rise and shine, it's breaking out time!" he announced. Alexander and Savannah jerked awake quickly, for a moment forgetting they were in the jail cell.

"Ah, Geoffrey, the person I want to have a word with!" Alexander declared. Cyrus reached deep into his pocket and pulled out a key but Geoffrey stopped him before he could put it in.

"Something wrong?" Cyrus asked.

"I just think everything should be explained before we let them out, so he doesn't kill us!" Geoffrey exclaimed. "So they can know what actually went on."

"Yes," Savannah said. "We were a bit curious about that ourselves!"

"So, obviously we had you captured—"

"We figured that much out, super star," Alexander said. *"Why* did you have us captured?"

REBELLION

"It was the only way to make it work," Cyrus started. "If it hadn't been for Lucerine, the original plan would've worked flawlessly, but with him here I couldn't afford to take certain risks. If you were going to fly into the city with my Rebellion army, then it was inevitable that the Alliance was going to counterattack."

"Obviously...tell me something I don't know," Alexander replied. Savannah smacked him lightly in the side.

"After I had you arrested, and with the help of Geoffrey, I pulled all my troops from the city to the outer-lands. I met with Lucerine again and he ordered that we start the attack on the city of Heldar early. I left with the Alliance troops.

"With Geoffrey at the helm, he used the Rebellion army to attack and destroy everything in the envoy. The only Dreygar that wasn't hit was mine. Then once I knew that Lucerine and company were gone. I sent some Rebellion soldiers to Heldar, but I brought the rest of the army here.

"As of right now, the city will be controlled by the Rebellion by the morning. The Alliance *did not* take over Heldar, but they don't know it yet! Lucerine thinks that I'm dead, making me a free man. I'm sorry for doing what I did," Cyrus said. "But it was Geoffrey's idea!"

"Oh! Hey! Thanks for throwing me under the bus!" Geoffrey exclaimed. Then the others stared at him as though he had done something wrong. "What?"

"What is a bus?" Cyrus asked.

"A bus?" Geoffrey asked, dumbfounded that they didn't know. "It's a bus. You know, it's yellow, with lights and...people."

"People with yellow lights?" Savannah asked, screwing her face up. Alexander looked at him with an amazed look.

"Your world is so weird," Alexander concluded.

"Back to the task at hand!" Cyrus instructed. He slid the key in the lock and swung the door open. Next he pulled out Sactalines and threw them in their direction. Alexander and Savannah tapped them and were clothed in their armor once again.

"I see we've ditched the Alliance disguise," Alexander stated.

"Yep, we're leaving and getting to Heldar so I can meet with Chrystar!" Cyrus said. They followed him down a twisting maze of tunnel and halls, until they reached a part that was so dark and dirty, they wondered if it was used at all. Geoffrey followed, but even he was beginning to wonder what was going on.

They turned one more corner and faced a small wooden door, which was no more than three feet high and two feet wide. Cyrus strode quickly to the door and tapped on it three times with the hilt of his sword. To their surprise the door creaked and groaned, revealing a tunnel that was completely dark.

"What is this?" Geoffrey asked.

"The Onlot Shaft!" Cyrus exclaimed. "The Onlots are an exceedingly rare sight. In fact in my time here, I've only see two of them. They are short and thin, and they are a tunneling nation of creatures. Over the centuries, they've tunneled across a good majority of the world. Now, we can use the tunnels and go wherever we choose as we see fit."

"Does the Alliance know about these tunnels?" Alexander asked.

"If they do, then I am not aware of it," Cyrus replied. "I'm sure Lucerine would have moved troops through them if he had knowledge of the tunnel system."

They stepped through the door, which Cyrus shut tightly and locked again. They began walking for about ten minutes, going deeper and deeper into the tunnels. Finally they came into a large space that looked to be nearly a mile across. A glass roof was above them and dozens of tunnels branched off to either direction.

REBELLION

In the center of the space, a single Dreygar waited patiently.

"How'd you get that in here?" Savannah asked.

"Not all the entrances to the Onlot Shafts are as small as the one we went through," Cyrus answered. He motioned Savannah to the pilot's seat.

"Which way am I headed?" Savannah asked as the great beast took to the air.

"The fifth tunnel to your left. With any luck we should be sitting on the shores of Heldar within three hours."

"How is that possible?" Alexander asked. "On land, it's several days from Merodia."

"I realize it doesn't make sense. I'm not sure exactly how these tunnel work, but it does only take three hours to get there." They all shrugged, deciding not to meddle on it any longer.

"Heldar, here we come!"

*   *   *   *

As Cyrus had predicted, three hours later they arrived beneath the city of Heldar. Savannah landed the Dreygar smoothly and they all looked around the darkened space they were in. The room appeared to have no doors or windows in it. In fact Geoffrey wondered if the city of Heldar was actually above them.

"Now what?" Alexander asked.

"I don't see a door," Geoffrey said.

"I'm not quite sure," Cyrus said. The others gave him a look. "I'm sure we're in Heldar because the wall says Heldar, but I've never actually been in this tunnel before."

"How did you even know which tunnel to take?" Geoffrey asked.

"One of the Onlots told me." They looked around the room for several minutes, finding nothing obvious. Defeated, they gathered at the Dreygar again. "Any suggestions?"

"How about this?" Geoffrey said, without warning he pulled his cross-bow and fired off several bolts at the wall where the name Heldar was inscribed. The wall exploded and to their surprise and relief the sight of sunshine and the smell of fresh air greeted them.

"Good job, Geoffrey," Cyrus gave him a pat on the back.

Meanwhile, Geoffrey stood in a daze, unbelieving. "I can't believe that actually worked!" he exclaimed. They fired several more, making the hole big enough for the Dreygar to walk through. They stood in a large open field; the towering walls of Heldar stood a half mile to their left, while large mountains loomed beyond that.

The grass blew gently in the breeze and the birds chirped, washing away all the past events of the war. For the first time in a while, they felt like a great burden had been lifted.

They walked for some time, not really heading towards the gate, but milling around in the fields. Some were filled with crops, others with wildflowers. Either way their hearts were lifted and their spirits soared as they laughed and talked together. At long last they glanced towards the large gate in the middle of the wall closest to them. To their surprise a man sat at the gate, smiling at them as though he enjoyed seeing the smiles on their faces.

Geoffrey relaxed as he noticed that it was Chrystar who was waiting for them. They made their way to the gate and sat down with Chrystar. Geoffrey's mind was put at ease about everything, as it usually was when

Chrystar was around.

"I'm glad to see all of you," Chrystar started. "Welcome to the city of Heldar, which on this day has not fallen into the clutches of the Alliance!" In turn, Alexander, Savannah, and Geoffrey all greeted Chrystar, but not Cyrus, who was quiet and appeared nervous.

"Cyrus Reno! It is a pleasure to meet you finally."

"It's a pleasure for me," Cyrus finally managed, appearing to be having trouble getting words to come out. "Forgive me, I'm rather nervous...and unsure what to do right now."

"What do you mean?" Chrystar asked.

"I've, just imagined about meeting you for so long now...I didn't know what it would be like. If I'd be able to talk, or if I would be speechless in front of the true king of the world."

"I understand," Chrystar said. "However, let me put those insecurities out of your mind, for they will not serve you well."

Cyrus smiled. "I suppose not."

"I would like to thank you for the mighty gifts you sent. The Sactalines are already being put to good use."

"I'm glad. I couldn't stand to see them in the hands of the Alliance any longer."

"Why?" Chrystar asked. The question clearly took Cyrus by surprise and even Geoffrey had to admit that it took him by surprise as well.

"The Alliance and I don't exactly see eye to eye on things."

"Did you once?"

"Yes," Cyrus answered. "At least I thought so."

"You *thought* so? Was that not the case?"

"Upon further reflection I can likely say that we never actually agreed with the Alliance."

"So what changed?" Chrystar asked. "What stirred your heart to turn against the Alliance?"

Cyrus thought hard for a moment. "No matter what I did, I couldn't shake the feeling that I was breaking myself with every order I followed for the Alliance. They said it was the way, but my heart and my spirit didn't agree. I was in turmoil, even though I shouldn't have been."

"So you didn't like what they asked you to do?" Chrystar asked.

Geoffrey hung on every word, wondering what Chrystar was driving at.

"It's more than that. It felt empty, worthless, like there was something missing."

"Do you still feel that way?"

Cyrus thought for a moment. "Yes."

"Let me ask you this," Chrystar said, now standing to his feet. "Why did you choose to gift all the Sactalines to the Kingdom? Why not give them to other groups or factions? There are, in fact, a lot of groups out there that don't like the Alliance."

"Yes, but through the presence of my brother and everyone connected to him, I have observed for some time now what their life is like and what love is like. I hated myself, but they did not hate me. They kept sparing me when we were in battle or not seeking me out for revenge, as they no doubt could have done."

"I see," Chrystar said. "It's from seeing the example your brother and people around him have given you. What is your intention of coming here today?"

"To join the Kingdom," Cyrus replied.

Geoffrey studied everything intently, but he hadn't see that one coming.

Chrystar smiled. "I can see in your heart that you speak no lie! This calls for rejoicing and celebrating, for one who was lost has been found." They all smiled, but Cyrus remained unmoved.

"Is that it?" Cyrus asked. "Can I join the Kingdom?"

"You already have," Chrystar answered. Both Cyrus and Geoffrey's faces both showed surprise.

"I have?" Cyrus asked.

Chrystar nodded.

"Are you sure?"

"Absolutely! There is no doubt in my mind about the condition of your heart."

"I thought it would be different, or require some great sacrifice on my part."

"Oh, it does! But maybe not in the way that you think. There is an element of sacrifice in every person who chooses to do something in my name. Your heart has changed, and with it you'll find that many other things also will change over time. Now draw your sword!"

Cyrus did as he was told and jumped in surprise as the blade, which should have had a red glow, now shone a brilliant white.

"Your sword reflects your heart. I know you wish to play both sides of the war, but it's an impossible task. One cannot serve two masters, for the heart will be divided. I require a heart that is pure, devoted, dedicated, loyal, and willing to lay down his life for one of his brothers. You may be able to keep your charade for a while, but that won't be possible for much longer, for when you are in the next battle everyone will see clearly, and where your heart lies," Chrystar explained. "Do you still wish to join us?"

"Yes," Cyrus said after a moment. "But what about a couple other things?"

"I already know that of which you speak," Chrystar assured. "Trust me, and the situation may yet turn in your favor."

Cyrus stood, looking amazed beyond words. He shook his head slowly.

"Is something wrong?"

"If you can help with those other things, then you're far more powerful then I ever thought."

Chrystar smiled. "Lucerine makes a good effort to distort what my true thoughts and feelings are, from the people under his jurisdiction. But when it all comes down to it, as much as he wishes to believe it...he doesn't know everything. He will never see this coming."

"Why not?" Geoffrey asked.

"He thinks it's impossible," Chrystar answered. "For a person to change and put aside their selfish ambition...he can't do it, so he doesn't think it can be done."

"I see things much clearer now," Cyrus said.

Geoffrey was startled when Chrystar turned his gaze to him. "And how about you, off-worlder? Do you wish to become a Chrystarian Knight?" Chrystar asked.

Geoffrey was surprised by the term being used, but for once he didn't mind. It sounded different coming from Chrystar, like a blessing rather than a curse as some people made it sound. "I thought I already had?"

"Geoffrey, one does not become a Chrystarian because their brother and sister-in-law are Chrystarians. Nor does a decision to follow me twenty years ago, and then never picking up a sword mean you are forever saved. You have to make the choice in your own heart. It is a choice. Every day when you get up. Many do not, and those poor souls fall into the clutches of Lucerine. Now I ask you...which is your decision."

"I've seen and experienced enough in the short time I've been here to know that I wish to be a Chrystarian," Geoffrey replied.

Chrystar smiled again. "Then there shall be much rejoicing and feasting tonight. However, I do have one request of you Cyrus."

"Yes, my Lord?"

"You have formed a mighty army, and their disdain for the Alliance is certainly strong. However, they have not yet had the chance to hear about me. Allow me to speak with them and see where their hearts truly lie."

REBELLION

Cyrus nodded his agreement.

At once, they went into the city and the bells rang loudly through the streets. Curiously, only the people from the Rebellion army came at the sound of the bells. Geoffrey pondered it.

Chrystar spoke to the assembly as he had spoken to Cyrus and himself, and everyone declared their loyalty to Chrystar. After that Chrystar led everyone out the north side of the city to where a great feast had already been prepared.

13

THE SUN WAS JUST beginning to come over the horizon when Roy finally put the truck into park. He looked at his passengers, seeing everyone else asleep. Abby and Christina were in the cab with him, while everyone else, including the others that they had picked up on the way, were piled together like a bunch of sardines in the back.

Roy struggled to keep his own eyes opened as he turned the truck off and carefully wiggled out from under Abby, who had fallen asleep on his shoulder.

The trees were filled with the sounds of birds, and dew gathered on every leaf. A quick glance around gave little indication of where the second door (if it was here) would be. He rubbed his eyes and grabbed a green Sactaline out of his pocket.

"Anyone out there? Gideon, Alexander, anyone?"

"Alexander, coming at you loud and clear," came the cheerful voice.

Roy smiled, feeling as though it had been an eternity since they had talked. "Glad to hear from you, my friend. I heard you were reunited with Cyrus."

"You must have talked to Gideon?"

"Correct. How's everything with Cyrus and Geoffrey?"

"For a while I wanted to smack them both upside the head, but it is now official that they are both on our side."

"Cyrus, too?" Roy asked.

"Yes. His entire army are now Chrystarians. It's a lot to take in, and I'm still trying to find out if it's real or not."

Roy agreed with that sentiment, falling silent for several moments. "So what are you up to now?"

"We just stayed the night in Heldar. Chrystar gave us the job of searching for slaves camps of some kind. Cyrus is familiar with them and seems to have an idea where they are, but doesn't know an exact location."

"Be safe, okay?"

"We will. Are Mom and Dad with you?"

"Yes, they are, and they've been doing just fine in this world."

"Glad to hear it. Your world is a little strange," Alexander said. "What else is new with you?"

"My cabin is gone."

"Gone?"

"Exploded. Big ball of flames."

"So how are you going to get back?"

"Chrystar said once there were three doors. We're currently searching for another one so we can get back to your world."

"Very interesting."

"We've also captured a Hentar Knight."

"Good job, Captain. Who did you capture?"

"The only name she's given us is Christina."

"Did you get anything interesting out of her?"

"She's very open. She also wants to join our side."

"Do you believe her?"

"She blew up an entire company of Alliance troops."

Alexander whistled in surprise. "I guess this goes to speak just how people of all ranks and society think of Lucerine and the Alliance."

"Indeed." Roy agreed. He turned to see Abby slowly getting out of the truck.

"Anything else I should know about?"

"Not really, just trying to get back to your world," Roy said. Abby came up next to him. "And your sister says it has been far to long since she's teased you, so don't die before we get back there."

"I will certainly take that under advisement!" The shuffling of feet could be heard.

"Don't worry, sister-in-law, I won't let him die. I'd like to keep him around for a while," Savannah said. They laughed.

"Well, love you guys, but it's time we go wake up our brother and get a move on," Alexander said.

"Hopefully we'll be seeing you real soon." Roy tucked the Sactaline into his pocket and greeted Abby with a kiss. "Sorry, no coffee this morning."

"How rude!" Abby said, with a wide smile on her face.

"However can I make it up to you, my dear?" They chuckled and looked around at their surroundings.

"How about we start by looking for a super secret entrance that's supposed to be here!" Jonathan called out. Slowly, everyone else crawled out of the truck. Jonathan helped Sylvia when she needed it, but for the most part she seemed to be doing well. Christina limped, but otherwise seemed to ignore all the pain she must certainly be feeling.

"I have no idea what we're looking for. Sweep the area, always stay with someone, and let's have armor and weapons, just in case," Roy said. Sactalines were handed out, and moments later they were in their uniforms. Sylvia was clearly astonished as the others tapped the sactalines, which to her must have looked like some form of magic. Roy pulled two spares Sactalines from his uniform and handed one of them to each Christina and Sylvia.

"I'm not sure I'm worthy to wear this yet," Christina admitted.

REBELLION

"I think you are, and besides if you die, you don't have the chance to become worthy, do you?" She smiled and said nothing further, only tapping the Sactaline and being dressed in the armor of a Chrystarian Knight.

"This is a bit much for me right now," Sylvia admitted.

"I'm sure it is," Abby replied, coming along side her. "Consider this though, all of the people from home got captured and this is the only way to hopefully find them and solve this riddle. Can you join us?"

"I can join you," Sylvia said. She tapped the Sactaline and jumped in surprise at the new armor. "I really have no idea what we're doing, though."

"Let's get started," Roy said to everyone, then he looked at Sylvia again. "I'm sure Jonathan can help you with anything you need." He noticed that both she and Jonathan looked down at the ground, a smile tugging at their lips. The rest of the team separated into three groups and began searching the forest all around them.

*   *   *   *

By the time midday came upon them, they felt they were no closer to finding an entrance then they were of stumbling on a lost pile of gold. The terrain was more difficult than they had expected, making it hard for Christina and Sylvia (and a few others who had light injuries) to keep pace and often meant that they had to wait until the others searched ahead to see if there was anything to investigate or not. Frustrating and annoying as it was, they continued in their search till it was nearly dark.

"Roy! I've got something!" a voice called out. Everyone hurried towards the sound, which was coming from an overgrown two-track.

Wiggs stood at the head of the trail and motioned to them.

"I'll be back in a couple minutes," Roy said. He and Abby quickly made their way over to Wiggs, who led them down the trail for nearly five minutes. The hills became large and steep, and with the fading light more and more was cast in darkness.

"How much further?" Abby asked.

"We're here!" Wiggs announced. Without warning they came into a large clearing, with trees bordering on all sides. They looked around at the clearing, not seeing anything that looked like a door. Wiggs noted their confusion and laughed. "You don't see it do you?"

He finally pointed to the very middle of the large clearing, where the shell of a horribly run down building sat on a crumbling foundation. Where once there had been a garage door there was now only a gaping hole. They hurried to it, pulling out a Sactaline for light as they peered into the building.

They carefully stepped into the old building. It creaked and groaned as a slight breeze moved through it. They let their eyes adjust to the lack of light.

On the back wall of the building, nearly a dozen boards were put together in no particular order, blocking off what lay behind.

They walked closer and studied intently. Behind the boards they could see a black chasm, much in the fashion of an old mine. On the front of the boards, there was one word written numerous times.

Chrystar.

"What do you think?" Wiggs asked.

"I think you might be onto something." Roy stepped closer, looking to the shaft beyond. "This building stands in the middle of a field, not against anything that would suggest a shaft leading anywhere. Good work, Wiggs.

let's get everyone else up here."

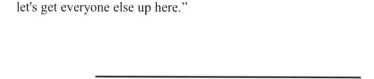

The next morning, Roy climbed out of their tent and met Abby by the fire, where she was warming herself. Everyone else was up, eagerly awaiting to explore the strange mine shaft. They had pulled the boards off and ventured down almost a hundred feet, until deciding they should wait until the next day to go any further.

"Ready to go, my dear?" Abby asked.

"As ready as I'll ever be," Roy answered. Victor and Norah stood with them around the fire.

"I'm still trying to wrap my mind around the fact that we found another entrance," Norah said. "It kind of boggles the mind doesn't it? Who made the doors? Where did they come from?"

"I guess the bigger thing to focus on is that it *is* here," Victor said. "Who knows the true history of these doors? It's anybody's guess. Or what their purpose is? You got me, but perhaps these doors were put here for this moment."

They nodded their agreement as Jonathan approached.

"Sorry to intrude, but can Sylvia and I have a word with you and Abby?" They excused themselves and followed Jonathan back to where Sylvia was sitting next to a small fire. She looked at them and smiled weakly.

"Here to listen, my friend," Abby said, sitting down with Sylvia.

"Not sure what I'm supposed to say," Sylvia said. "I have this horrible growing feeling that I shouldn't go into your world."

"I see."

"I'm not sure why I feel this way, but I've had nightmares about it since I learned of a second world. I'm not a warrior, I don't know a thing about fighting, should it come to that. What is my purpose in all of this?"

"I'm not sure I can answer that for you," Abby said. "But what is being pressed on your heart?"

"It sounds so selfish, but I want to go home. To *my* home. To Granville. I want to run my store and see the town prosper again!" Sylvia said. "How am I supposed to do that if I'm in a different world?"

"Our first mission is to the find the people who were kidnapped *from* town," Roy said. "We can figure everything out, afterwards."

Sylvia nodded her agreement, and Abby stayed and talked while Roy and Jonathan slipped away.

"What are your thoughts on this?" Roy asked.

"Conflicted," Jonathan admitted. "I'm not sure what my role will be in the coming days. If we get back, and if we manage to find everyone from the town, their wounds will not easily heal themselves."

"I know," Roy said. "Abigail and I talked about that last night. Together we thought that if we find everyone and can get them back to this world that perhaps, you should stay with them."

"I had been thinking the same thing, and not just because Sylvia and I have taken a liking to each other."

"I know," Roy replied.

"I'm not sure what I should do."

"You don't have to decide now. I can tell you see the bigger picture. If we get through everything and get everyone home, you certainly have our blessing to stay with the town and help them through everything, if you so choose."

Jonathan smiled and nodded his thanks.

Twenty minutes later, everyone was assembled at the old shack. Sylvia and Jonathan stood together. Christina and Abby walked alongside Roy. They entered the shack and soon the entire company was swallowed by darkness. The outside light vanished and everyone pulled out Sactalines for light as the path in front of them grew darker and steeper.

Once inside, the shaft opened up and seemed to have multiple other paths that went here and there. They walked for nearly an hour, as some places it became so steep that they struggled to keep their footing. Christina had the hardest time out of all of them, but refused to rest or take a break. She seemed to have something on her mind, though she didn't say what it was.

Finally, the path leveled out and became smooth running up to a large opening within the shaft. In front of them three tunnels opened up, seeming to head in completely different directions.

"This is unexpected," Evelyn said from behind.

"Can't say I was expecting to see three different tunnels," Wiggs said. The others all agreed. "What now, Captain?"

Roy thought for a moment. "We split up," he announced. "Jonathan and Sylvia, lead the group to the left tunnel. Abigail and myself will take the right tunnel. Evelyn and Christina, if you wouldn't mind exploring the middle tunnel. The rest of you, split yourselves up and follow us." Within seconds the groups were all sorted and they headed into the different tunnels.

14

FOR THE MOST PART, the tunnel to the right was easy traveling. It gently climbed and then descended a number of times, but there were no major obstacles, and overall they made good time. The team walked for about an hour in silence before they came to a door frame followed immediately by a large piece of black stone.

"A dead end?" David asked.

Roy and Abby looked closer. "I'm not sure," Roy finally admitted. "It looks like there should be a door here, but I'm not sure how we're supposed to get that stone out of the way."

"What if we shoot it?" David asked.

"Granted, that would solve one problem, but I can think of another problem," Abby said. The others chuckled. Roy and Abby pressed their ear up against the slab of rock and motioned the others to be quiet.

"This stone isn't that thick," Roy whispered.

"Can you hear something?" one of the others asked.

"Shuffling of feet, sounds like someone is getting a drink of water," Abby answered.

David looked unconvinced. "A drink of water? Where does this door lead, to a lake?"

They ignored the question and spent the next half hour trying to push the stone or come up with some other way to move it. When they had exhausted all of their ideas, they sat down on the floor. Abby pressed her ear to the door.

"Any more noise?" Roy asked.

"I don't think so," Abby replied. "We've been making quite a ruckus in here, I'm surprised the person on the other side hasn't heard anything."

"Are you sure the person is still there?"

Abby nodded. "I can hear a creaking chair. A rocking chair."

"You can tell what kind of a chair it is by the creak?" David asked in astonishment.

"It's a very distinctive creak." Abby answered. David looked at Roy in disbelief.

"She does have exceptionally good hearing," Roy said. "She claims we have a stair on our porch that creaks slightly differently than the rest of them."

"We put that to the test once and what did it reveal?" Abby asked, already smiling.

"That you were right."

"That I was right!" Abby exclaimed. "And I'm right about this, too." Roy's smile turned to anxiety as he spotted the grin on her face.

"No. No, no no! That's a bad look!" Roy exclaimed. Abby gave him a sly smile.

"Back up, people. It's time to have some fun!"

"Good Lord help us all!" Roy exclaimed. Abby grinned like a child on Christmas. "Back it up people."

"Does this bring back memories, off-worlder?" Abby asked pulling out her crossbow.

"Yes, it does! That was the most frightening way to meet a person."

"I feel like we need to hear this story," David said,

"If we survive, I'll tell you!" Roy said. He hurried them back through the tunnel a safe distance and ducked for cover. Abby fired a single shot at the slab of rock. To their surprise, the rock appeared mostly unaffected with only a one-inch indentation in the surface. They studied the rock, eventually noticing a small, barely visible crack that ran from top to bottom, down the middle of the rock.

"Abby, do you think you can hit the same mark twice?"

"I'll give it my best shot!" Abby exclaimed. They laughed. "Quite literally."

They backed up again and she fired three more bolts. A thin stream of light now ran up and down the slab of rock. They celebrated, but then were hushed by the sound of a baby crying. Confused and concerned, they worked together and were able to part the two slabs of rock enough to squeeze through.

They found themselves standing in what would've been a very lavish but homey dining room. Straight ahead of them was the kitchen. A baby's cry echoed through the house, as well as the sound of someone frantically trying to hush the baby.

"What did you do?" Roy whispered.

"What did I do?! Last I checked you told me to fire at the stone slab, *Captain*!"

"Can't argue with that, can I?"

"You're not going to win, that's for sure," David said as he crawled through the opening. The baby quieted down and for a moment they heard nothing.

"See? The baby's okay!" Abby whispered. "Lets try and figure out where we are. David, you and Carmela guard the entrance."

They began to move but were stopped when the red glow of a Hentar Blade was leveled at their heads.

"Stop where you are!" a woman cried out. Her voice was frantic and the sword in her hand was shaking. They looked beyond the sword to see a middle aged woman, with greying brown hair. Fear filled her eyes and she seemed to be fighting back tears. They straightened a little. "Don't move! Please!" the woman begged. "I don't want to kill anyone!"

"You don't have to," Abby said calmly. The woman seemed to understand, but not completely accept what she said as truth.

"Yes, I do," the woman defended. "My master gave me strict orders. If anyone comes while they are gone, I'm supposed to kill them."

"I'm not sure who your master is, but we're not here to hurt you," Abby said. Roy was amazed at her calm voice and how clearly the other woman was comforted by it.

A moment passed until finally the woman burst into tears and dropped the sword.

* * * *

Evelyn and Christina led their group down the middle tunnel, amazed at the size and scope of it. The tunnel was really (in Evelyn's mind) more like a grand hall. The roof was nearly three hundred feet above them and wide enough they could've fit several Griffins in side by side with room to spare.

The further they walked the more they realized that they were descending lower and lower, but into what they didn't know. The time passed slowly as they were forced to take several breaks for Christina's sake.

"Are you sure you want to continue?" Evelyn asked. She could see in her face that she was clearly winded.

"Yes, I'm sure," Christina replied.

"If you need to take a longer break, we can."

"No." Christina pushed herself to her feet. "I need to do this."

Evelyn didn't press the matter any further, and they started off down the tunnel again. The floor was smooth, though occasionally dotted with massive boulders that they had to go around.

They walked for several more minutes, taking note that there were large buildings now carved into the cliffs. Soon they turned into towering structures leading from the floor all the way up to the very top of the cavern they were in.

"I wonder what this place used to be called," Wiggs said.

Evelyn looked at everything in wonder. "I'm not sure, but maybe this tunnel between the worlds had much more traffic in the days of old," she said. They walked through the forgotten city, which sprawled everywhere. Bridges and towers, battlements. Everything a city would've had was built here under the mountain.

They came to a stop when in front of them, as far as the eye could see, was a chasm. Despite the chasm, the buildings that they had been walking through remained, appearing to be floating in air. On the other side, far in the distance they could see light.

"Any ideas?" Christina asked. Evelyn gave them a smile and pointed up above them. When they looked they noticed thousands, if not tens of thousands of small cobblestone bricks floating ten feet above their head.

"I've seen these before," Evelyn replied. "They're called Umarian Bricks. It was defense mechanism of old days. If your enemy was coming and you didn't want them to enter your city, they would float in the air. If they were your friend, the bricks would come to your aid."

"Nice," Christina said.

"Unless you're in a position like we are...we have no idea what this city was like. Who would have been considered a friend? Who would have been

REBELLION

considered an enemy?"

"Why do you think this city is in between worlds?" Christian asked.

"This is a place that is reserved for special use only," a deep gravely voice said from behind them. They looked to see a man dressed in a brown tattered robe. He carried a staff in his hand and his beard came down to his belt. Though his appearance was rough, his eyes showed life and gave them comfort.

"What kind of use would that be?" Evelyn asked, carefully studying the man. He smiled as if he already knew how to answer that question.

"The kind that seeks not for their own gain. I know you, and I know your hearts. I can tell that you do not seek the door on the other side for yourself, though you do want to go home. In the deepest parts of your hearts and minds, I can see a concern and conviction that could move mountains."

"I'm not sure I understand," Christina said.

The man smiled. "I know, my child, I know. But she does." The man turned to Evelyn and held her gaze for a moment. "In time I'm sure all will be made clear to you. Now, take a step of faith and see if you aren't saved!"

They looked at him in disbelief, but in an instant Evelyn understood what he was asking and leapt out into the dark pit. To her relief the cobblestone bricks raced from their spots and formed solid ground beneath her feet.

Christina and the others did the same, cautiously moving around, wide smiles stretching across their faces as they began playing like little school kids.

"This is amazing!" Christina exclaimed. "How can we ever thank you, sir?"

"Get to the other side and do it quick!" the man answered. They wasted no more time and started walking through the city again. The others finally reached the other side, but Evelyn looked back to find Christina still

134

standing in the middle of the large expanse. Evelyn walked back out towards her.

"Is everything okay?" Evelyn whispered. Christina didn't respond, she just kept staring at the stranger on the other side.

"Who are you?" Christina called out. The man seemed to smile.

"I am." In an instant the man vanished as though he had never been there. They turned and headed to the landing where the others were anxiously waiting.

They now stood facing what looked like a door, but it was actually a hundred feet tall and nearly just as wide as the cavern was. They walked forward and ran their hands along the doors. The doors creaked and groaned, swinging outwards all by themselves.

They were blinded by a swift sunrise and the sight of battlements as it appeared that they were standing in the midst of a great fortress. To either side of them and coming to meet in the middle was a large wall, and then a gate. From beyond, they could smell salt water.

Without thinking about it, they stepped out onto the gap. More cobblestones rushed to their feet and made a path for them to walk. They came up onto the wall and looked behind at the sheer cliff they had come through. Christina's eyes came alive and soon a joyous laugh came from her mouth.

"What is it?" Wiggs asked. Christina laughed again and wiped a joyful tear from her eye.

"I know this place!" She ran ahead to the edge of the wall, looking out over the ocean beyond and took a long deep breath. "I've missed the smell of the ocean!"

"How do you know this place?"

"I used to play here as a kid. I used to live just over that hill. Mother and Father would bring us here to play. This is the ruins of Pintair!"

"Sounds like fun."

Christina smiled from ear to ear. "Oh, it is!"

"I'm not familiar with Pintair," Wiggs said.

"It's been forgotten by everyone. Even Father discovered it by accident when we were kids."

"It's a nice view, but how is this going to help us?" David asked. Evelyn thought hard for a moment.

"I'm not sure," Evelyn replied. "But I think we were meant to find this place for a reason."

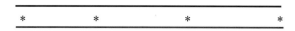

Jonathan couldn't believe how narrow the tunnel had gotten. When they had first parted from the others, the tunnel had been nearly fifty feet in width, now it was down to single file, and threatening to get even smaller. The distance above their heads had also shrunk, to where many of them had to bend down to get through.

Sylvia walked directly behind him, willing herself to go on. Jonathan's heart broke with the fact that things from a different world had caused her pain. He helped her when she needed it, but otherwise she seemed to be doing just fine. The tunnel wasn't nearly as bad for her, as she wasn't the tallest person he had ever met.

Another hour passed as they walked in silence until the tunnel became so narrow they had to turn sideways. They came at last to a large cavern. It was no more than twenty feet across in any direction, but compared to the

136

small and narrow tunnel, it felt like a mansion.

They took a small break before starting off again. The tunnel continued on the other side, being no more roomy or spacious than the previous tunnel. At the end it widened into another room which was much like the first one they had rested in. In the far wall was a plain wooden door.

Jonathan crept to the door and grasped the handle. To his surprise it moved exceptionally easy. He pulled the door open only a crack, surprised to find that it weighed much more than it should. He and Sylvia peered out the door, seeing a large clearing and forest beyond. In the clearing were thousands of tents. Surrounding the clearing where just as many Alliance troops, crossbows in hand and swords hanging by their sides. They studied the sea of faces. Sylvia's mouth opened in shock as another group of people were paraded by their secret door in chains and tattered clothes.

Jonathan gently placed his hand over Sylvia's mouth and pulled the both of them back enough to push the heavy door shut. Finally the handle clicked and they both sunk down to the ground.

"What did you see?" Wiggs asked. The other's with them peppered them with a hundred questions.

"What did you see?" Jonathan asked Sylvia.

"Everyone from our home," Sylvia replied. Mr. Jensens. Miss Davenport, Mr. Cartwright and his wife. My father was there as well. They've all been captured?"

"Yes, and forced to fight for the Alliance if we don't do anything." Everyone fell silent.

"How many people were in the camp?" Wiggs asked.

"My best quick estimate is five thousand," Jonathan said.

"Five thousand?" Sylvia asked. "Are they're all from our world?"

"It would be safe to assume so, but we can't be certain about anything. What we need to do is-"

"Get them back!" Sylvia interrupted. "We need to get them back."

"We will, we will," Jonathan reassured. "I'm not sure how, but we will."

"Maybe Roy would have an idea."

Jonathan shrugged and pulled out a Sactaline, laying it on his lap.

"Roy, you out there?"

"I'm here, Jonathan. Glad to hear from you. What did you find at the end of your tunnel?"

"People. A lot of people. Perhaps mostly off-worlders like yourself."

"Interesting."

"What did you find on your end?"

"It's been interesting to say the least, hurry on back and we can all compare notes. There's a lot to discuss and try to figure out."

"Yes, sir." He put the Sactaline away. "Five minutes and we head back, everyone." The others nodded and kept to themselves, leaving Sylvia and Jonathan alone.

"I'm not sure what to make of your world," Sylvia said.

"To be fair, we are in a middle of a war. It's a much nicer place when the Alliance isn't involved."

"I'm sure it is. What's this war being fought over anyway?"

"At the core of all the battles and facades...people." Jonathan said. He had never truly thought about it before. "This isn't a war about cities, or territory, or liberties of people. The Alliance holds people in chains and forces them to do their bidding, as you've just witnessed. They have no regard for people, and will do whatever they can to maintain their control. It's only been in the past year or two, they've openly declared war on the group that stands against them."

"The people you fight for?"

"Yes. We're called the Kingdom."

"Nice ring to it," Sylvia replied. "What does the Kingdom stand for?"

"Freedom. Choice. Love. Specifically love for ones enemies."

"How do you love your enemies?"

"By reminding yourself every day that you're not fighting them...you're fighting against the ideas that drive them. For the most part, you can't blame the Alliance soldiers or citizens for their actions, because they believe what they've been told or taught. They're not bad students, they just have a bad teacher."

Sylvia nodded and pondered the meaning. "So unconditional love?"

"Yes and no."

"What do you mean?"

"Chrystar, our leader, will take in anyone, no matter what your condition. No matter where you are in life. However after you join the Kingdom it is assumed and perhaps expected that you will try your best, with his help, to rid yourself of those destructive habits and thought patterns. It is no small task, but with Chrystar anything is possible."

Again silence fell over them.

"I don't know if it would be allowed, by my heart still loves Granville. But I also feel a strong leading to do some good in this world and help in whatever way I can. Is there room for one more in the Kingdom ranks?" Sylvia asked.

Jonathan smiled.

15

"**COME ON! WE'RE** almost there!" Cyrus urged. They trudged through the tall grass, which in this case was far over their heads.

"What kind of grass is this?" Geoffrey asked, having never seen grass like this before.

"Perimu Grass," Cyrus answered.

"Of course it is," Geoffrey replied, sarcasm dripping from his voice. "And how in the world of tall grass do you know there's a slave camp nearby?"

"Long story, so I'll give you the short version," Cyrus started. "The Alliance had been secretly working on various varieties of tall grasses and thorn bushes as a natural defense."

"What good is that going to do against Griffins?" Alexander asked.

"Griffins were never the focus. It was a way to keep slaves or groups of people from escaping. Plant a combination of them thick enough and you could starve people into submission or do whatever you wanted in a town."

"I don't understand. We can still get through this tall grass easily enough," Savannah said.

"Yes, but the height of it would deter most people. Full grown, this goes up to twenty feet high. And it grows thorns and barbs that are poisonous. Plus, I'm willing to bet-"

140

They all stood in awe as an entire wall of thorn bushes stretched in either direction as far as they could see. The thorn bush itself was nearly thirty feet high.

"This is new," Cyrus said. "The last time I saw this place, the grass was all that was here. I was able to spot it from the air."

"So that's how you knew there was something here?" Geoffrey asked.

"Yeah. After that I broke into the senate chambers in the middle of the night and found papers confirming my theory. Since then, I've made regular high passes over the area and watched it grow."

Cyrus grabbed hold of the giant thorn bush and began pulling himself up. The others followed suit.

"How many people do they have?" Alexander asked.

"This camp has about five thousand," Cyrus answered. "Unlike the other camps, I know this one is one hundred percent off-worlders."

"How do you know that?" Geoffrey asked.

"Other nighttime raids, some disguised as the Alliance, and others on my own time. Every person I saved came from this camp. All of them are off-worlders...that's a fact."

They finally reached the top, only going far enough to look over the top into a sea of tents and bodies. Geoffrey looked in horror as thousands of people were forced into lines and given orders. It only took a few seconds to know that if they refused, they were whipped or tortured.

"How do you plan to get these people out?" Savannah asked.

"I'm not sure," Cyrus admitted. "Chrystar told us to do this, so there's got to be a way, right?"

"Can't argue that," Alexander agreed.

"Look at that cliff on the other side," Savannah pointed, and they all strained their eyes. "A crack just appeared in the cliff."

"A crack?" Alexander asked. Even Geoffrey looked closer. After a moment he thought he saw it until it vanished again.

"I saw it," Goeffrey said. "It seems to have disappeared though."

"Cyrus how much do you know of maps of this area?" Savannah asked. They began making their way through the tall grass again, noting that it had grown ten inches since they had come.

"To my knowledge there isn't anything beyond those cliffs. None have ever traversed them before," Cyrus replied.

"Then you know what I'm thinking?"

"You think there's a door to the other world there?" Alexander asked. Savannah nodded. "I would never guess it, that's for sure."

At that moment Alexander held up a hand and pulled out a Sactaline that had been growing hotter in his pocket.

"Hello?" Alexander said.

"Alexander! Good to hear from you!" Gideon joyfully greeted. "Did you find a camp?"

"We found it and now we don't have any clue what to do about it," Cyrus declared.

"Well, I've got other news for you," Gideon began. "Roy and the rest of the A-Team have made contact. They found an old shack in the woods that led to a tunnel with three entrances. Each one brings you to a different areas. You can join them if you can get yourself to the ruins of Pintair. Roy seems to think the door there will be easiest to get through."

"Cyrus, do you know where that is?" Savannah asked. He nodded.

"I can get us there."

"Great!" Gideon's reply came. "Don't waste time. Get yourselves there, and chime me in when you arrive."

"Yes, sir," Savannah replied. "We'll make for the ruins as soon as we get in the air."

Geoffrey's heart was conflicted at the thought of going home. He might have only been in this world for a short time, but already he felt like he was part of this world, or that it was part of him. Would he really be able to go back if he had the chance?

They climbed aboard their Dreygar and were lost to their thoughts as they took to the sky.

"Do you know anything else about this region?" Alexander asked.

Cyrus shook his head. "Afraid not. My wife would know more than I do. She grew up in these parts."

"Your wife?" they all echoed.

Cyrus smiled happily. "Guess I forgot to tell you that."

"I'll say! No wonder you were not wanting to join the Kingdom right away. You didn't want to reveal that to us!" Alexander exclaimed.

"I'm in a tight spot. My wife is high up in the Hentar ranks, but completely disloyal to the cause."

"What's her name?" Savannah asked.

"Christina."

*   *   *   *

Almost an hour later they landed at the ruins of Pintair. They slid off the Dreygar and walked through the remaining trees until they followed a large ramp that led to the top of the wall.

"This is one of our favorite spots," Cyrus commented, pointing to the ocean view from atop the wall.

"It is beautiful," Savannah said. "Where are we supposed to go now?"

"I thought someone would meet us here."

"Don't worry. We wouldn't leave you hanging!" a voice yelled. They turned to see Victor and Norah coming out of a large gaping hole in the castle ruins. Cyrus was taken aback. They greeted each other with embraces and smiles.

"Good to see you again, Geoffrey!" Victor said, shaking his hand. Geoffrey smiled, understanding perfectly what had transpired between everyone here.

"It's good to see you, son," Norah said, smiling from ear to ear.

"Glad to be here," Cyrus said. "I've been here many times and I never knew there was a door here."

"Roy has several theories on that. The leading one is you'll only see it if you're looking for it."

"Seek and you will find?" Geoffrey asked. Norah nodded. Geoffrey pondered it, knowing it could be true. "Well, whatever the reason, I feel very blessed to see the door."

"More talk later. Let's hurry up and get back," Norah said. "Roy would also like us to try and fly the Dreygar through the door and cave."

"Savannah, do you mind?" Cyrus asked.

She smiled. "All aboard!"

They followed her and quickly climbed onto the Dreygar which launched itself into flight. Savannah led them out over the ocean, doing a dive and skimming the surface just for fun. Geoffrey looked out on the world, a hint of sadness overcoming him. He hoped he would get to come back and help in this battle.

Savannah turned hard and lined up for where the door was. They flew closer and closer at incredible speed. Alexander rode next to her white-knuckled.

"Hon!? What do we do if the door doesn't open?!" Alexander exclaimed. Geoffrey's mind was beginning to also ask the same questions. They still sped towards the door, but Geoffrey knew, even now, they wouldn't be able to stop in time.

"If it doesn't open, then it was nice knowing you!" Savannah cried. They all cried out as they struck the rock, only to find that they were greeted with a flash of light, followed by darkness and a new tunnel that they hadn't expected. All of them let their cheers echo through the new tunnel.

An explosion shredded the peaceful morning as everyone in the camp jumped to arms. They relaxed a moment later, seeing the white shack, destroyed, but now able to see a large Dreygar circling overhead. Roy smiled and was quickly joined by Abby as they watched the rest of the team cheer for the new arrivals.

Savannah gracefully landed the Dreygar and everyone rushed to them. Roy watched the sight as everyone talked and laughed joyfully. Geoffrey slid off the Dreygar and came over to Roy, embracing him with a wide smile.

"Good to see you, brother!" Geoffrey said.

"Good to see you, too!" Roy replied. "Maybe next time you'll listen when I say not to go upstairs?"

Geoffrey smiled. "It was an interesting experience, that's for sure. Overall though, I didn't find it particularly hard to adjust to the other world. I rather liked it over there and in some ways I'm saddened that I had to leave."

"I understand," Roy said. "But as I've come to realize, things tend to come together just the way they're supposed too."

"Any predictions for the future?" Geoffrey asked. Roy shook his head.

"Yes, one actually, and we'll probably find out in two minutes." Geoffrey's face showed so much surprise and confusion that Roy couldn't help but crack a smile.

"What? You're not going to tell your brother?"

"Let's just say there's not time to fully explain it-"

"Well! Well! Well!" a voice echoed through the air, instantly halting the celebrations that had been going on. They looked to see a big burly man with an unkempt beard plodding his way towards them. A sinister smile was on his face and a chuckle rose in his throat.

"What do I have here?" the man gloated. "High ranking members of the Kingdom? And if I'm right, I've ensnared the A-Team. The *famous* A-Team! I wasn't trying to get you, but needless to say, this will be a profitable day for me."

"Axil," Cyrus said plainly. "To what do we owe this pleasure?"

"You can dispense with the ignorance," Axil said plainly. "I was assigned to keep an eye on you for the last several months. Seems our beloved leader didn't quite believe all the numbers on your reports, regarding certain Sactalines out of Merodia."

"Axil is a low-laying, skiniving snake," Cyrus told them.

"Says one who was supposed to have been killed by their master."

"What do you want?" Roy asked, sternly.

"To take anyone with the name of Van Doren to Lucerine himself!"

"And you think you can just walk in and take us?" Abby asked.

Axil laughed. "Yes."

"Rather bold," Roy critiqued. "I assume you're referring to the team that we found in the woods last night?" He nodded and David, pulled open one of the tents to reveal twenty people tied and gagged. Axil shifted only slightly.

"I don't even know who they are!" Axil insisted. "I was talking about this team."

As fast as Axil's people could reveal themselves and pull their weapons, they were struck by bolts from all of Roy's team, including the members that were stationed out of sight. The bodies slumped to the ground.

"Those people?" Roy asked

"It's war," Axil replied plainly. "It appears the A-Team is as good as I've been told! Very, well. If all of you won't come, then I highly recommend that Mr. Cyrus Reno does! If he ever wants to see his little girl again." Axil noted their surprise. "Oh, has he not told you he has a little girl?"

Roy stepped forward. "Sorry."

"For what?" Axil asked.

"For what's about to happen."

In an instant, Axil was knocked to the ground and disarmed. When he opened his eyes next he was looking up the blade of a sword, with a faint white glimmer to it. Confusion was written all over his face.

"Christina!" Cyrus called out.

Roy held him back.

"Tarjinn?" Axil asked.

"Not anymore," Christina replied.

A sly smile came to his face. "I think I understand now...you never killed your apprentice as you told everyone—you became lovers! In that case I warn you...I can kill that baby girl in an instant, and tell Lucerine everything about what's transpired."

"You could, but you can't." Christina replied.

"Why not?" Axil asked.

"Because we have the baby girl," Roy said. Right on cue, the middle aged woman they had scared the previous night came out of another tent, a baby girl in her arms. Fear came over Axil's face.

"I'd kill you myself," Christina started. "But I'm not a person who kills in cold blood anymore. Furthermore, I think it'll be far more fitting to let you crawl back to Lucerine and tell him how you failed him. Let's see how forgiving he is."

Several members of the team came and bound him tightly and the rest of them breathed a little easier. Cyrus and Christina both rushed to each other and then to their baby girl.

"How did you manage to find both of them?" Cyrus asked.

Roy smiled. "We have a lot to catch up on."

16

"**I CAN'T THANK** you enough for everything you've done," Cyrus said. The celebration has subsided and now only a few of them remained awake to figure out their next move.

"I wish we could take credit for everything that transpired, but with the way that everything fell together, we can hardly take credit. It was perfectly designed," Roy said.

"Even I understand that now," Cyrus replied. "I suppose I've always known that the Alliance was corrupt. But with the way they treat and educate you...it's hard to come out of it and not be in agreement with the Alliance."

"What first caught your attention?" Abby asked.

"Christina, or Tarjinn, as she's known professionally."

"How's that?" Geoffrey asked.

Cyrus thought for a moment. "She saw something in me that I didn't see in myself. The first time we met, she said I would've made a horrible Hentar Knight, but she hadn't been looking for the qualities that would normally be sought after by the Hentar. She wanted to work against the Alliance, but was trapped. So she found me, and ever since then we've been trying to secretly undermine the Alliance in any way we can."

"And falling in love with her?" Abby asked.

Cyrus chuckled nervously. "It came slowly, but I think that's how love should be."

"I agree with that," Evelyn said, breaking her silence. "The slow love is the best one because it doesn't happen via, big events, but all the small little things that over time pile up into big things. It is best when you fall in love with a person's character as opposed to their status or physical attributes."

They fell silent, each pondering Evelyn's words in their own way. Roy and Abby could certainly relate to having fallen in love slowly. In his mind there was nothing ordinary about their story...but it was a good one and they both smiled at the memories throughout the years.

Roy looked to Christina, who had fallen asleep next to the fire. Their baby girl was snuggled up next to her. Looking at her now, Roy could hardly believe that *she* was Tarjinn. They had battled it out dozens of times, and it was no secret that Tarjinn was considered one of the best Hentarian Knights in the Alliance.

"I'm in debt to you," Cyrus said. "Truly I am. It was an answer to my prayers when I showed up here and saw Christina. And then to find out you had found my daughter, Cassidy, as well? I couldn't believe what I was seeing."

"At the time we had no idea there was a connection," Abby explained. "We had been exploring another branch of the tunnel you came through. We blasted through a rock wall, and accidentally scared the wits out of your nanny. After that it only made sense to take her with us.

"When we got back, of course, Christina immediately recognized her daughter, and the secret that you were the husband was certainly a surprise, but a welcome one."

"So the tunnel we flew through went to my house?" Cyrus asked.

"It branched off to three passages," Roy explained. "One went to your house, the second went to Pintair and the other one went to a slave camp of some kind."

"I know where that slave camp is. In fact, Savannah thought she could see a door opening."

"She might have seen Jonathan, then," Abby said.

"We have to help the people in that camp. That camp specifically," Cyrus said.

"Why that specific one?" Evelyn asked.

"That camp is for off-worlders," Cyrus answered. "None of them asked for this, or even knows what's going on. They need to be set free. Chrystar told me to see them free."

"We can get behind that," Roy said, thinking carefully. "Would the plan be to bring them back to this world?"

"I don't see why not? Maybe we can help them get home," Cyrus suggested.

"It's going to take a lot of provisions and supplies," Geoffrey said.

"More than we have," Evelyn pointed out.

"Is there no way?" Cyrus asked. Roy watched his face, for the first time realizing that in every aspect that Cyrus's heart had indeed been transformed. He smiled at the difference.

"What about the door Savannah saw? The tunnel?" Geoffrey asked.

"We caved it in," Abby said. "Both of the other entrances were destroyed. We couldn't risk anyone discovering the doors. Besides that, the tunnel for the slave camp was too small to do anything."

"So if we're going to rescue everyone, we have to get all of them to Pintair?" Geoffrey asked. "That's going to be impossible."

"Never tell Chrystar the odds," Evelyn said.

"Does anyone have any idea on how to get everyone from the camp to Pintair? It's a great distance and I'm sure they'll be noticed if they're missing," Abby said.

"I have an army...well, now they're part of the Kingdom," Cyrus answered. "But I am still appointed as their commander."

"Higher rank than any of us!" Abby exclaimed. "I guess we have to take orders from him." They all laughed.

"The only problem I see is that we have to get all of the slaves through the door and destroy it before any Alliance troops give chase. And furthermore, everyone who's involved in this operation is not going to be able to go back until we find the third door into the world," Roy said.

"It's going to be difficult," Abby agreed.

"Difficult, but possible?" Cyrus asked. "I know this sounds like a crazy objective."

"The best things always are," Abby said. "Besides, we're the A-Team, we're not about to be normal."

"Sister, I think you're the poster child for 'not normal'," Cyrus teased. They all laughed again.

"Like you are," Abby retorted.

"Shall I try to contact Gideon?" Evelyn asked. They nodded their heads and she pulled out a Sactaline. After several attempts he finally answered, sounding rather groggy as though he had been woken from a deep sleep.

They quickly filled him in on the events of the past couple days, including the news of their new allies, Cyrus and Christina.

"Chrystar informed me of that," Gideon said. "I'm glad to hear that we're all on the same team again. I know that's always been a hard one to deal with."

"Sorry if we woke you," Evelyn said.

"It's quite alright, my dear. I've been busy doing research on possible doors, while still keeping up with all the other work and meetings that need to happen in war."

"Anything new?" Roy asked.

"The Alliance was completely defeated at Heldar. They made a very strong effort to destroy the city, using the mines beneath it, but they were unsuccessful. Gryn and Jumar have fallen to the Alliance, but there are plans to counter strike and hopefully get the people out. In other news, Cyrus, your scout teams have located four more camps of recruits or slaves. How many did you say there were?"

"To my knowledge, there were only six. Even Christina doesn't know where the sixth one is. Although she entered Roy's world through it, she was for the most part unaware that she was going through it. I do know that's the biggest one."

"We'll save that for later," Gideon said. "I like Chrystar's idea of rescuing all these people, but you're not going to take them all to the real world, are you?"

"No, only off-worlders would come here," Roy replied. "Cyrus says that camp is solely for off-worlders."

"That's right."

"Any idea how many people are in the camp?"

"Probably five thousand," Cyrus replied. Silence followed for a minute.

"Okay. First, you need to tell me what kind of supplies you'll need," Gideon said.

"Tents, food, Sactalines, for starters," Roy said. "All of these people and supplies have to enter through Pintair."

"That will make things a little harder."

"If you can come from the Tunlet Sea, you'll probably be unseen by everyone," Cyrus said.

"I'm not familiar with that area," Gideon admitted.

"It's filled with hundreds of small islands. Small enough and unimportant enough to not be a concern of the Alliance," Cyrus told them.

"Thanks, I'll look into it!" There was a pause as they could hear a shuffling of papers. "How do you expect to get these people out?"

"I was hoping to use the soldiers from my former army to free the people," Cyrus said. "Does Chrystar approve that?"

"I don't know, let's see!" They heard Gideon put down the Sactaline and walk a few feet away. Though it was faint they could still hear what was being said.

"Chrystar? Hey, man! Wake up!" The sound of a pillow smacking someone reached them.

"I'm awake! I'm awake!" Chrystar's voice exclaimed.

"Cyrus is wondering about using some troops to rescue slaves," Gideon said. They could hear the two of them coming closer to the Sactaline.

"Greetings, friends!" Chrystar said. "Sorry, you caught me taking a slight nap. Everyone needs those every now and then. You should certainly take a large number of troops to aid in your mission. However, there are some things you need to do first."

"Name it," Evelyn said.

"First, you need to make a sweep of the other towns and villages in your mountains. I'm thinking you'll find them empty. If they are, it will work to our advantage."

"How's that?"

"Because we can inhabit them," Cyrus said. "If people are from these towns, it'll be like going home."

"Exactly," Chrystar said. "Now, I do warn, that there is a rare chance that when you destroy the second door, we will not be able to contact you like we are right now."

"Really?" Roy asked.

"It's a little fuzzy," Gideon replied. "But from all of our research the two doors you've found so far were spots that were occupied by people previously. Try as hard as I can, I have yet to find any documentation on the third door."

"So be prepared for every scenario when we pull this off," Geoffrey said.

"That's correct," Chrystar told them.

"Just my unprofessional opinion," Geoffrey started. "But if you're going to pull off a heist of this size, you're going to need sufficient distractions in order to get them looking away."

"Agreed," came the reply. "Gideon and I have been talking about this for a while, and I think we have some things planned that will be sufficiently distracting for the Alliance. With any luck Lucerine won't know what hit him. Let us know when you search the surrounding towns," Chrystar said. "Is there anything else?"

"Yes, actually. One more thing," Roy started. "A few people we've run into seem to be actively looking for me or Geoffrey. Do you know anything about that?"

"Suspicions, mostly. With all the stuff Gideon and I have been reading, we've mostly concluded that only people who own the entrances can activate any of the entrances. Therefore because *you* bought the cabin, you can see the door. But not everyone can."

"But the Alliance seems to have found one," Evelyn said.

"Yes, this is true. But Roy has been an active member of both worlds, so they appear. Therefore, people like Roy, and Geoffrey by extension are very important to him. If he can turn one of them to join the Alliance, then he would be able to secure all the knowledge about the doors and discover their secrets, and he likely thinks he'll be able to control the doors for all eternity."

"Interesting," Geoffrey and Roy both agreed. "So he wants us for the sake of controlling the doors?"

"Partially," Chrystar replied. "There's a little more to it, but I gave you the simple version."

"The simple version will do just fine for the moment." Abby said.

"In that case, be careful and let me know what you find out!" Chrystar said.

"We will," Evelyn said. "Gideon?"

"Yes, my dear?"

"Stay safe. I love you, and hopefully we'll get to see each other soon!"

"I love you, too," Gideon said. The Sactaline went silent, and Evelyn put it into her pocket.

"Lets get some sleep, everyone," Evelyn said. "We have a long couple of days ahead of us."

Everyone dispersed to their tents. Abby fell quickly to sleep, but Roy was unable. He went back out to the fire, which to his surprise was still roaring. Cryus sat with his daughter Cassidy in his arm. Roy smiled at the sight.

"How do you like being a father?" Roy asked. Cryus smiled.

"Just as much as I enjoy being a husband," Cyrus replied. They were silent for a moment. Finally Cyrus looked at Roy knowingly.

"What's on your mind?" Roy asked.

"I have one more secret to tell you, and then a humble request, but first I need to know that I'm speaking to you in confidence," Cyrus said.

"Your secret is safe with me," Roy said.

"It's about those innocent people I sent into your care when the war started."

"The three girls?"

"Yes."

"Who are they?" Roy asked.

"Christina's younger sisters," Cyrus answered. Roy nodded, finally understanding. "That rescue mission I was supposed to get her entire family out, but they were the only three left."

"This might further explain why Christina said she was looking for us," Roy reflected. Cyrus nodded.

"I don't know what to expect or even what to ask for... I'm sure it would do Christina's heart good to see them again."

"I understand everything now," Roy said. "Lets get the next few days over with before we decide anything, or make anything known. The girls are safe where they are...right now this place isn't safe."

"I agree. Thank you."

*　　　*　　　*　　　*

The next three days had been some of the busiest that the A-Team had ever experienced, as far as the amount of jobs to be done and the amount of people they had to do them. The morning after their conversation with Gideon, Savannah had been sent into the sky, carefully flying the Dreygar as she searched for any sign of life among the other towns and villages. From there, the rest of the team had been split up.

Roy and Geoffrey had taken the truck back to the site of the former cabin and had quickly gotten Geoffrey up into the air, in his plane, to help Savannah search the areas that they thought might be still occupied and would be freaked out at the site of a Dreygar flying overhead. From there, Roy, Sylvia, Jonathan, and a few of the others made their way to Granville where they opened the airport for Geoffrey and filled his plane with fuel as often as it was needed.

By the end of the first day, they had fixed the necessary things in the town, enough to accommodate what they had in plan for the small, usually forgotten, town.

The second day, both Geoffrey and Savannah reported that nearly all the towns and villages for nearly three hundred miles had been emptied. By the end of the day it had been increased to nearly four hundred miles. The news certainly helped them to relax as it gave them some breathing room, and didn't have to worry about being seen by anyone.

The camp at the second door was expanded and near the end of the second day large shipments, brought in by Dreygars and Griffins alike where dropped in the open field. Some of the supplies were sent to Granville, and the rest were kept at the camp. They worked through the night to set up the thousands of tents and unpack the food that had been sent for their soon to be refugees.

In the third day Roy and Cyrus went to look at the improvements and reinforcements at the site of Pintair. The city had become nearly as bustling and productive as it had been back in its day. The people who had come, were only here to help the defense of Pintair and wouldn't actually be stepping foot into the real world at all.

This came as a surprise to some of Roy's team members, but for the most part no one seemed to mind or particularly care. Each seemed perfectly content to play their role in the coming rescue mission.

Between the numerous meetings and strategy that went along with planning an operation of this size, they still found time to have fun and relax. Every night they would sit around their campfire and talk until they fell asleep. This night was no different.

"It feels good," Cyrus said, awakening all of them from their daze. "To be on this side of things."

"I'm glad," Roy said. "Are you nervous?"

"Are you?" Cyrus countered.

"I always get nervous before a mission," Roy stated.

"Chrystar is with us," Cyrus said.

"Yes, but he does not promise that we will live," Geoffrey pointed out.

"That's right," Evelyn said. "What does he say?"

"For I know the plans that I have for you. Plans to prosper you and not

to harm you, plans to give you a future and a hope," Alexander said.

"Good. And what does that mean?"

"That there's a bigger picture. Chrystar can see it, we can't," Alexander replied. "We need to trust in that bigger picture, because he believes in us."

"Very good," Evelyn replied. "Always remember every one of you has been put here for such a time as this. It did not happen by accident."

"That's one thing I've been thinking about a lot," Christina said, breaking her silence. "How do you know it's not an accident? Many people, if they knew, would say that my becoming a Chrystarian, or being found by Roy in the first place *was* an accident."

"They may say that, and to many it may look that way, but what about you? Did you intentionally seek out Roy? Did you wish to become a Chrystarian Knight as soon as you heard the name?"

"No. I was just following orders," Christina answered. "I suppose there was always something inside of me. Deep inside of me that told me of the wrongs in my life. I shouldn't have looked for an apprentice like Cyrus, but I did. I never thought I would find an apprentice who would measure up."

"You see?" Evelyn said. "It was something...deep. Inside you. If everything had accidentally happened you wouldn't care. But, Chrystar sought *you* out. Calling you to a better life. Now that he has your attention, you get to join his 'big story'."

Christina smiled. "Never thought about it quite like that before. Sure puts things in perspective."

"Yes, it does."

They fell silent and said their good-nights, with each party returning to their perspective tents. Roy and Abby remained by the fire for some time, looking up at the stars.

"Big day tomorrow," Abby said.

"Yes, indeed. A lot of moving parts."

"Are you worried about tomorrow?"

REBELLION

"A little anxious I suppose."

"Here to listen."

"We're rescuing people from a war, while hoping not to attract attention and bring the war to this world, while others are going to be fighting a battle in an actual war as we try to save people. And in the end of it, we have to get everyone through a cave in the fortress of Pintair."

Abby laughed. "When you say it like that, no wonder you're anxious! Relax as much as possible and take a deep breath. We just have to focus on our part of tomorrow, and then we'll see what comes afterwards." Roy nodded, knowing she was right. They got up and went to their tent and sleep came over them.

17

THEY HAD BEEN up before the break of dawn, making final preparations and now, finally, they were nearly ready. Roy put his truck in park and stepped out to greet the rest of the team who were assembled and waiting. Geoffrey also climbed out of the truck, putting one final box of supplies in the back, should it be needed.

"Good morning everyone," Roy said. They returned his greeting. "Big day, if everything goes to plan we'll all live to tell about it." Roy took a deep breath, facing the group that was with him. In the front were the members of the A-Team, while behind him was a great number of generals and pilots ready to get started.

"Final role call, Go!" Roy said into a Sactaline. "Jonathan and Sylvia?"

"Good to go."

"Cyrus and Christina?"

"Good."

"Alexander."

"Good."

"Savannah?"

"Good sir."

"Gideon and Evelyn."

"Good."

"Traceadox and Wiggs?"

REBELLION

"All's ready in Pintair."

"Okay, pilots to your Dreygars or Griffins, whatever the case is. Jonathan and Sylvia, wait until the time is right, for the rest of us this is a time sensitive mission. Cyrus, you're first."

"Copy." Cyrus replied, half in a whisper. A minute or two later everyone was in position and signaled that they were ready.

"All-right. Here we go. Five...four...three...two...one...go!"

*   *   *   *

Cyrus took a deep breath, trying to calm his nerves. Christina noticed he was nervous and so far they had kept each other from going crazy. When they drew swords this time, there would be no turning back. Every Alliance soldier would recognize them and realize that they had joined the Kingdom.

For the past two days, the former Rebellion army, (which were conveniently dressed like Alliance soldiers) had been slowly filtering into the city of Citalia. For the most part, the operation had been smooth and uninterrupted. The city of Citalia had been under control of the Alliance since the beginning of the war, and it was clear no one in the city suspected anything.

Snow filtered down through the air and a cold wind threatened to eat right through the two of them. The city was high in the mountain range, maybe twenty miles from the slave camp.

"Are you afraid?" Cyrus asked.

162

"Surprisingly, not right now."

"How are you not?"

"I've spent years being afraid of being found out, for not being loyal to Lucerine and the Alliance...but I didn't know what else to stand for. Now I know."

Cyrus marveled at her words and felt his own faith grow as they waited.

"Cyrus, you're first," Roy's voice rang through the Sactaline.

"Copy," Cyrus said in a whisper. He nodded to Christina who gave the command to everyone else in the city, via a different Sactaline. Their army of nearly ten thousand strong was placed strategically through the city, all of them were on foot.

"All-right. Here we go. Five...four...three...two...one...go!"

In an instant, a cry went up throughout the city as everyone with Cyrus and Christina cast off their cloaks and began attacking the Alliance troops, who for the most part were completely surprised and confused, as the people attacking were also dressed like they were.

Cyrus felt his energy surge and his fear vanish as his confidence grew with every swing of his sword. Bolts lit up the city in bright explosions; some of them were blocked and others struck people who didn't have armor on.

Cyrus and Christina fought side by side, slowly pushing towards the citadel at the middle of the city, which was built entirely of ice.

"Do you think our plan is working?" Cyrus asked.

Christina peered intently up to the top of the citadel. "Commander ran in! They're in a panic!" she yelled above the noise of the explosions.

"Response team at Yumar was just sent your way. ETA: five minutes." Gideon said through the Sactaline.

"Savannah, don't let them reach the city!" Roy's voice commanded. "Alexander, your turn!"

REBELLION

Alexander took a deep breath and faced the menacing cave entrance in front of him. David followed him, step by step, and looked nearly as nervous as he was.

"Are you sure we're going to find them here?"

"Cyrus said they keep almost two hundred of these things in this cave."

"How do we know they'll attack the city and not us?" David asked.

Alexander thought for a moment. "We don't?"

"We don't?"

"In theory, we have to get behind them, scare them out of the tunnel, where they will then go pummel the city."

"But they could still turn and maul us?" David asked.

"It's possible."

They said nothing else as the tunnel of ice began to glow a deep red, dark at first, but growing steadily until the entire ice tunnel was illuminated as though it was daytime.

At last they came to a great hall, nearly two hundred feet wide. To either side of the hall, standing nearly twenty feet tall, were monsters they had never imagined. David stared in shock and disgust.

"They're even uglier and weirder than I thought!"

"Same here," Alexander said, taking in the strange creatures. They were tall and covered almost completely with unruly, tangled hair. The light that filled the tunnel came from the strange creatures as they appeared to be on fire. Flames consumed them, but they never burned and obviously never felt any pain from it. Their feet and hands held great talons, which looked as though they could easily pierce through ice as though it was nothing more than a piece of paper.

"Close the gate!" Alexander said. David quickly shut the gates they had just walked through. Alexander held his cross-bow at the ready as they carefully crept by many of the sleeping giants. Soon they came to the middle of the grand hall where many gates branched off in numerous directions.

"Cryus said the fifth gate?" David asked.

"Fifteenth," Alexander corrected.

"I was close."

"Yeah, sure."

They counted the fifteenth gate from the left and quickly made their way to the large gate. They lifted the metal latch and pushed the gate open. To their surprise it swung open without difficulty and without squeaking. They turned back to the sleeping giants.

"How do we wake them?" Alexander asked.

"You're the brains here," David said. "You didn't think about this part at all?"

"Not really," Alexander admitted. He walked up to one of the furry beasts. "Hey, you! Bigfoot! Wake up!" The sound echoed through the tunnel but otherwise there was no change.

"Good job," David said.

Alexander shot him a look. "Do you have a better idea?"

Without hesitation, David aimed his cross-bow at the wall behind the creatures and fired off two bolts. The arrow exploded in a ball of fire and instantly all the creatures woke with a vengeance. Alexander and David both cried out as they frantically tried to avoid being crushed by the great beasts who were angrily trying to figure out what had happened.

"Scare them awake. Great idea!" Alexander yelled above the noise.

REBELLION

The giants instantly stopped, every head turning towards him. They growled menacingly.

"Yelling so loud they can hear," David whispered. "Also a great idea." They remained frozen in time as Alexander was afraid to move and the giants seemed to be processing what they were seeing. One by one, the monsters started inching their way closer.

"Better idea," Alexander said, in a strained whisper. "We run!" Alexander sprinted through the hall, with David hot on his heels. To their horror, their plan actually worked and all the monsters gave chase. Alexander and David slid into the tunnel that they had opened. The monsters paused for a moment and then charged down the tunnel after them.

"That's right, take that you looser! Come and catch us!"

"Weird monsters coming down the tunnel. Coming in hot!" Alexander yelled into the sactaline with him. Despite all the chaos on their end, the only reply Alexander heard was Roy's calm, voice.

"Copy that."

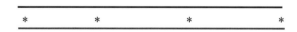

Savannah flew at the head of the great host of Griffins and Dreygars. Over five hundred of them, each with twenty soldiers aboard. She looked straight ahead, waiting for their enemies to appear on the horizon.

"Savannah, have you spotted them yet?" Roy asked.

"Negative," she replied. "Wait! I see them."

"Let me know how it goes in a few minutes, okay?" Roy said.

"You got it!" Savannah replied. She taped a different Sactaline from the spot in front of her. The Sactaline was green, and grew brighter.

"Remember everyone, make your shots count. We'll try and direct them to the plateaus. Most importantly, we can't let any of them reach Citalia." The Sactaline was filled with countless, 'Yes, ma'am's' and 'Copy that'.

Within moments, the entire squadron had arranged themselves in formation. By now it was evident their enemies had spotted them. They sped towards each other, waiting until the other was in range.

"Fire!" Savannah yelled. The entire sky was filled with the flashes of arrows in a great arch as they dropped onto the backs of their enemies. A bright flash of light radiated through the sky and they could see many dark shapes falling towards the ground.

Soon, return arrows were fired. They braced for impact as the sea of arrows came overhead. One soldier aboard every Griffin reached into their pockets and threw a magenta-colored Sactaline into the air. They sailed up overhead and then exploded. The first volley of arrows that had been shot at them, were detonated but took none of them out.

"That was the easy part, now for the hard part!" Savannah said. She flew confidently, glad to have her Griffin, Dawnchaser, joining her in battle this time. The two sides met in the sky, a flurry of arrows and explosions rocked the airspace.

For a few minutes it seemed all they could see was explosions as the armor on everybody's uniforms and creatures were quickly spent. They reached into their reserves and put a new set of armor on creatures and themselves as needed. Some fell to the ground, unable to get new protection on in time.

They pressed forward, the enemy circling back around and firing on them from behind. Savannah looked ahead seeing another group of Dreygars coming directly towards them.

"When I say, everyone dive to the ground!" Savannah yelled. They all maintained their course as three different groups of Dreygars closed in around them. The flash of arrows being released caught her eye and at once, without her saying everything, they dove to the ground in unison. Instead of hitting them, the arrows struck the other Dreygars, taking out many of them.

Savannah breathed a sigh of relief, letting everyone else return to the sky, while she flew just above the forest floor, looking for their destination. The entire area was filled with massive plateaus of rock that she had mentioned. She located them in the distance and circled back towards the main group.

"All groups, follow me!" Savannah yelled through the Sactaline. She pulled out an orange Sactaline and held it in the air. The light grew, creating a stream behind them, signaling everyone to her location. Every Griffin followed and so did the Alliance.

They sped towards the plateaus, blocking off endless arrows and attacks from behind them. The arrows increased and several of the Griffins began to fall.

"Come on!" Savannah said to herself. "Only a little further." A moment later, they reached the top of the first plateau and her heart sank. Where Kingdom soldiers were supposed to be waiting to support them, instead they laid their eyes on dead bodies. Bodies were slain everywhere and soon Alliance soldiers filled the ground below and began firing on them.

Dawnchaser cried out in pain as an arrow penetrated in the chest where the armor had been destroyed. Everyone aboard clung on tight as they plummeted towards the ground.

*　　　　*　　　　*　　　　*

"I can't get Savannah on the Sactaline," Abby told Roy.

Roy thought hard for a minute. "I've tried four or five times." He tapped a Sactaline in front of him.

"Traceadox and Wiggs, are you still with us?"

They had put a second squadron of nearly two hundred Griffins only five minutes from the plateaus in the event that they were needed.

"Yes, sir," Wiggs replied.

"Savannah's squadron is in trouble. Assist them in anyway you can and take out every Dreygar you come to. Find out what happened."

"Yes, sir," came the reply.

"Alexander, what's your status?"

"Trying to stay alive!" Alexander cried. "Why did you choose me for this task?"

"Because you can run the fastest," Roy replied. Abby chuckled.

"I'm going to get you for this!" Alexander complained. "Hopefully we'll be free from this tunnel in two minutes!"

"Good. Cyrus and Christina, what do you have?"

"We're pressing for the citadel, the city panicked initially, but we don't know if they've called for any more people."

"Got it. Jonathan and Sylvia, what's happening at the slave camp?"

"Nothing of significance," Jonathan replied. "Is Savannah and the squadron in trouble?"

"Maybe, we're not sure right now."

"If the Alliance did eliminate the entire squadron, Citalia isn't going to call in any more reinforcements," Abby commented.

Roy nodded. "Okay, I know this will change some of our plans but I think it's time. I'm going to bring this squadron to attack Citalia. The squadron from Pintair will join me."

169

REBELLION

"Doesn't that leave Pintair a little light on defense?" Sylvia asked.

"I don't see we have much of a choice. I'm flying to Citalia, as soon as you two tell me that they've pulled a majority of the troops at the slave camp. I'll break off with the two hundred-fifty Griffins we planned on and head back to you. Sylvia will have to unite them. We'll come in, it'll be a quick smash and grab, we'll load up and get out of there."

"Sounds good. We'll stand by," Sylvia said.

"You doing alright, Sylvia?" Abby asked.

She sighed heavily. "I'll do better once everyone is safe. I'm not used to this notion of war."

"We understand," Roy said.

"I have to add, this is a side of you I never knew existed," Sylvia said. "I always thought you were some kind of a spy, but never pictured you as a commander."

"Technically, Gideon's still the commander," Evelyn chimed in, teasingly. They all smiled.

"Thank you for the compliment," Roy said. "We'll get everyone back safe as soon as we can." He tapped several more Sactalines that were lined up in front of him. They lit up brighter. "Gideon is going to assume full command for the duration of the mission." Roy tapped the Sactalines and all except one went dim. "Gideon, we're headed up."

"Be safe."

"We will." Abby said.

Geoffrey looked at them both and smiled. "Now, my brother, are you ready to come to a strange new world with me this time?"

Geoffrey smiled. "Yes, that sounds like a lovely idea. What did you have in mind?"

"Certainty of death, with a seemingly small chance of success?"

"What are we standing here for? Let's go fight in a war!"

They both turned and headed towards Skyquill as all the other pilots began boarding their Griffins.

Abigail walked next to Roy, stifling a smile. "Brothers."

18

ALEXANDER FELT AS though he would die of a heart attack before he reached the end of the tunnel. The monsters roared noisily behind them, doing much better at navigating the ice tunnel than he and David were.

They quickly ducked around another corner, catching their breath for a fleeting moment as they monsters slid past the corner they had gone around. They began running again, panicking when a wall of ice rose up in front of them.

"Nice knowing you," David said.

Alexander stared at the wall in confusion. "This can't be the end of the tunnel!" he cried. The monsters had now corrected their course and were thundering down the tunnel towards them. In nearly a full blown panic, both David and Alexander grabbed their cross-bows and fired arrows at the end of the tunnel. Flames filled their sight, but then gave way to a frigid breeze and a vigorous blizzard.

The monsters paused for a moment, as if they didn't remember what the outside world looked like. Down below they could see the icy, frozen city, engulfed in war. Anger and rage came over all of their faces and they talked in a strange language amongst themselves for a moment.

The giants hardened their expressions, glaring at Alexander and David who were completely unsure of what to do. The leader of the giants roared noisily, the entire mountain trembling at his voice. He thrust his claws into the side of the cave and pulled off a tremendous piece of ice from the wall of the tunnel.

"Alexander?!"

"Just jump!"

They both jumped off the ledge, free-falling the seventy-five foot drop to the mountain below. All they could see overhead was large projectiles flying towards the city.

*   *   *   *

Christina angrily fired back at anything that moved. The fighting had grown harder and more intense as they had pressed towards the citadel. Behind her, Cyrus lay up against the wall with an arrow stuck in his side. Blood flowed from the wound. They had been cornered in a small bunker, meant for the defense of the city, they could hold out for a while, but they couldn't last forever.

"Gideon!" Christina called through the Sactaline. "Anything you can do to help?"

"I've sent everyone we have in the city to your location. I can't do much more from here," Gideon said.

Christina felt her heart sink. She looked back at her husband who was struggling to maintain consciousness. His expression was blank and her hope began to waver.

A thunderous roar shook the city and in an instant large chunks of ice could be seen falling to the city. She watched as they pummeled through the walls as though they were toys, and continued rolling for some

173

distance. She jumped back and dove for Cyrus as one of them struck the ground near their bunker. It made a horrific sound as it crushed the wall to bits, bounced slightly and shredded the roof of their bunker.

Their sight was blocked but when the snow and flurries had settled they could both see the devastation of the city. Christina brushed herself off and then looked into Cyrus's eyes. She glanced to his side and pulled the arrow out of him. He cried out.

"It doesn't look bad," Christina said. She was lying and she could see in his eyes that he knew it too.

"Go, Christina," Cyrus said, in almost a whisper.

"No! I'm not leaving you here."

"Go!" he said more forcefully. "They're distracted. Get to the citadel and talk sense into the leaders!"

"I can't leave you!"

"You need to! Think of the others. They need you."

"I'm not leaving you!" Christina cried.

"Think of the others!" Cyrus urged. "Think of our daughter! Fight for her. I'm broken, and whether I live or die, I will be too much of a hindrance to continue any further!"

"No!" Christina said, sobs preventing her from saying anything else.

Cyrus closed his eyes hard and seemed to be struggling for each breath. "Do this for me!" he pleaded, the words nearly inaudible over the sound of the battle. His head bobbed and then he went unconscious. Christina cried bitterly as she held her husbands hand.

She was pulled from her sorrow as the blast of an arrow knocked her backwards onto the hard snowy ground. She quickly stood and grabbed her crossbow. A group of soldiers came down the stairs to her left. She fired and struck every one of them. She hurried to them, grabbing their black Sactalines, which would give her all the arrows that she needed.

"Christina, are you still with us?" Gideon asked.

Christina heard, but didn't reply. She ran forward, taking out anyone who came her direction, holding back her tears as she did.

She pressed forward. The arrow fire increased, but still she continued on, grabbing whatever supplies she could, armor, or weapons, from the people she had taken out. Time slipped away from her until finally the citadel gate was in sight.

She ran around one last building and was struck across the face by a long staff of ice. She stumbled backwards and fell to the ground, her bow sliding out of her reach.

"Go ahead! Reach for it! Dare you!"

Chills ran up and down her spine as she looked into the eyes of an angry and desperate Axil. He grinned sadistically.

She began to sit up, but was struck by the staff again.

"That's for making me look like a fool!" She began to move and he struck her again. "That's for your betrayal!" She laid on the ground, blood coming from her lips. Pain coursed through her. "And this one," Axil nodded to two people who lifted her up, "is from Lucerine and the Alliance!" He struck her in the ribs and she fell to her knees gasping for breath.

"That's right. I'm sure you've got a couple ribs that are broken and your face will likely never look the same," he taunted. "And trust me, I can do far more than that to you, if it's called for." The soldiers with him formed a circle.

"Behold the great Tarjinn!" Axil jeered. The others laughed and then mocked her.

"What's this going to prove?" Christina asked. The fact that she had said anything seemed to catch them off guard. "That you can beat up an unarmed person?"

"No!" he kicked her in the chest and she fell back. He stooped over her. "It'll prove that nothing can save you. Where is Chrystar now?"

REBELLION

"Where's Lucerine?" Christina snapped. "Where is your great leader? You've proved nothing!"

"I've proved that I'm loyal," Axil snapped. "What can be said of you?"

"Loyal?" Christina replied, struggling to get to her knees. "You laid waste your entire family for the Alliance."

"They were traitors and needed to be dealt with! You of all people should know that!"

"Have you no compassion, no mercy?" Christina managed.

Axil scoffed. "Only a weak, spineless, piece of flesh like yourself would entertain such thoughts. What would it gain me to show them such things? Why have rules if you won't enforce them?"

"You have to enforce rules! I'm not arguing that. You ask what it would gain you to show them compassion and mercy? It would gain you nothing and that's where your corruption is complete. You think only of yourselves. You don't think of the Alliance, and certainly not Lucerine. Maybe you haven't met him but I have, many times. You're a tool to him, not a person. Not a human being." Her face stung as she was backhanded.

"You watch that tongue or I will cut it right out!" Axil thundered.

"We've known each other since we were kids...I'm not about to willingly let you continue to destroy your life! I've learned that no matter how you justify it to yourself, you can't silence the voice in your own head. When you're alone. When you have a bad day. When all you want to do is talk to someone who will listen. Despite all the training the Hentar are given about how we're independent and don't need people, we all cling to community...almost like a creator made it that way."

Axil's face turned vile as he grabbed his sword and rushed towards her. Christina closed her eyes, expecting to die, but instead the clash of metal on metal came to her ears. Her heart leapt with joy and alarm as Cyrus stood in front of her, having blocked the blow. His injuries were obvious and already he seemed to be overcome by the pain. Axil attacked again, easily knocking the sword from Cyrus and then kicking him in the side where the arrow had been. Cyrus fell onto the ice.

"Men, ready your bows. I was supposed to take both of you to Lucerine, but I think you fought too hard and ended up killed as we tried to capture you. Isn't that right boys?" Everyone affirmed what he said. The bows were raised and the soldiers stood ready to shoot when ordered.

A loud thunderous sound rumbled through the sky. They looked up the mountain, seeing a large chunk of ice being thrown down onto the city. It crashed twenty feet away, bouncing and rolling towards them. Axil cursed as he jumped out of the way. Several of the men were killed, but otherwise the group was uninjured.

"Leave him and bring her!" Axil yelled. Christina was yanked from her spot and bound. She searched for Cyrus, seeing him still laying on the ice. His eyes were open and shone with life, but somehow faded. They picked her up and left the city.

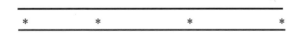

Roy flew with the other Griffins all behind him. Abby and Geoffrey rode with him and other than that they were by themselves. Each of his squadron only had two people aboard most of the Griffins as they had expected to be heading into a rescue situation, not a battle. The Griffins and Dreygars from Pintair were the only ones armed with the minimum ten bowmen atop each of them.

"What are your orders, Captain?" one of the other pilots asked.

"Intermix the armed Griffins with the unarmed. All we're going for

REBELLION

here is distraction. We need to scare the city leaders enough that they call for the majority of the people at the slave camp."

"Copy that."

"If you see someone in need, stop and help them, but do it swiftly. When I give the signal, we have to go."

"Yes, sir." everyone replied.

"You okay, hon?" Abby asked.

"As okay as I can be. I'll be glad when this battle's over."

"Don't worry. I'm right here beside you, all the way."

Roy smiled.

"And I'm here with you too!" Geoffrey exclaimed.

"Glad to hear it." He turned towards the sactaline in front of him. "Gideon! Do we know where Alexander ended up?"

"Yes, he and David are as they said, 'stranded' on the north side of the city, near a gaping hole in the mountain. I can't give you a more detailed description than that though."

"It's okay, It sounds pretty self-explanatory," Abby said.

"Anything else?" Gideon asked.

"Any word on what Traceadox and Wiggs have found?"

"Nothing."

Silence plagued them for a moment.

"Anything else? I've got five other people wanting to talk to me."

"Sorry."

"Don't be. You're just much better at handling all of the different sactalines than I am," Gideon replied with a laugh.

"Just like a switchboard."

"Off-worlder reference?" Evelyn pipped in.

"Yep."

"Gotta go!" The Sactaline went dim.

"I hope Savannah's alright," Abby said.

178

"Me too." Geoffrey replied. They didn't get a chance to talk anymore as the city came into view. They descended out of the sky, flying low and spread themselves over the entire city. Anyone who could, fired arrows. The arrows grabbed the attention of the their enemies, who hastily let their arrows fly. By the time the arrows reached them, they had passed.

They wound their way through the streets, avoiding the battle overhead, while distracting any troops that were on the ground. Quickly they could see that panic was beginning to spread.

They flew over the citadel and felt chills run through their skin. They could see in the distance a large line of fiery monsters. Behind them, barely visible, they could see two people huddled up against the rock, where there was indeed a gaping hole in the side of the mountain.

"Cyrus!" Abby yelled. She pointed to the ground. Roy and Geoffrey both spotted him. Roy immediately changed course, descending rapidly. They landed amidst the wreckage, Geoffrey and Abby jumped off and stooped over her brother.

"He's alive!" Geoffrey yelled back.

Horns blared through the city and a tremendous sound shook them to the core."

"Bring him. We have to go."

"Jonathan just confirmed that most people were pulled from the slave camp!" Gideon's voice came through the Sactaline.

Geoffrey hoisted Cyrus over his shoulder, running him to the Griffin.

"Good. Execute procedure twenty-two," Roy responded, helping to pull Cyrus aboard.

"Procedure twenty-two?" Gideon asked. "I'm not familiar with that." In the background they could hear Evelyn already starting to carry it out.

"File out in alphabetical order, thirty seconds apart, heading in the opposite direction you need to go. No one will notice you that way." Skyquill pushed off into the sky again.

REBELLION

"When was that made? I'm not familiar with it, but Evelyn seemed to know what you're talking about."

"We'll discuss it later," Roy said, leaving the conversation as they were forced to navigate a large bombardment of ice chunks as the fiery creatures threw them and then proceeded to charge the walls. They climbed high and then went into a steep descent, landing just feet from Alexander and David, who climbed aboard even as they were taking flight again.

19

"THERE THEY GO," Jonathan said. He and Sylvia sat on a high cliff overlooking the slave camp. Below them was the entrance they had been at the other night, the tunnel for that door was completely destroyed.

They remained where they were. In a matter of minutes hundreds of guards and overseers alike loaded onto Dreygars and took to the sky.

"I'm amazed they took so many," Sylvia remarked.

"Looks like we have about fifty to deal with," Jonathan replied. "Then the hard part."

"Convincing them to listen to us?" Sylvia said.

Jonathan nodded.

"My father will be an easy one, but he won't command the respect of everyone," Sylvia said.

"Who do you need to find?"

"Gary Duman. He's got connections of every kind in dozens of towns in the mountains. He's well respected by many. If I can get him to listen, he can get the rest of them."

"You sure you're up for this?" Jonathan asked.

"No, but we don't have a choice," Sylvia said. She had mostly recovered from her injuries and Jonathan knew that she wouldn't be content to sit back and do nothing. Still he had to admit to himself that *he* didn't want anything to happen to her.

REBELLION

"All teams get ready," Jonathan whispered through the Sactaline. "Take out the guards but nobody else. Understand?" Everyone replied. They had stationed nearly five hundred people all around the slave camp, some of them a half mile away, while others were spaced out on the same cliff they were on.

"How far is it from Citalia to here?"

"We have probably fifteen minutes until the first Griffin arrives and then they're going to come quickly." She nodded, seeming to get lost in a thought she had.

"What happens when this is over?" Syvlia asked. "When everyone gets back to their homes?"

"I'm not sure," Jonathan admitted. "Though I've thought about it plenty."

"What were your thoughts?"

"I feel conflicted," Jonathan said. "I feel like I should fight in this war, but in the same time I feel like I need to stay with the people. In some strange way I feel like that will be how I fight in the war."

"What do you mean?"

"They've been through things and seen things that no one in your world has ever dreamed of. Life will never be the same for them, they just don't know that yet. I feel responsible for them, almost as if they're my own people."

"So you would stay in my world?" Sylvia asked. Jonathan thought hard for a moment.

"Yes. There is another reason too," he said with a smile. Sylvia looked away, trying to hide a smile.

"We're in position." a voice whispered through the Sactaline.

"Go," Jonathan replied. In a flurry of activity every soldier on the outskirts of the camp jumped from their hiding spot and quickly threw down the Alliance soldiers, and then stood in their place. Jonathan and

182

Sylvia crept to the edge and threw a rope over.

Together they crawled over the edge and descended to the barren, dry ground of the slave camp. They were unseen by nearly everyone until they touched down on the hard ground. Every head was turned towards them and murmurs when through the crowd as they stood and looked to their guests, who were dressed in the armor of the Chrystarians Knights, which had not been seen by them.

For a moment everyone was silent.

"I'm seeking Gary Duman!" Sylvia yelled to the crowd. Still silence followed.

"Gary Duman!" Jonathan called out. Finally there was murmuring in the crowd as a man, in his late fifties stepped out of the masses and came forward.

"Sylvia!" Gary exclaimed. He paused a moment later, clearly recognizing her face. He turned behind him. "Henry! It's Sylvia!" At once, her father came up and wrapped her in a firm embrace.

"I thought I had lost you." her father sobbed. "For the love of all that is good in this world, can you please tell me what's going on?"

"It's a complicated explanation," Sylvia said. Her father's eyes still begged for it to be answered.

"Perhaps in this case, they may need to hear all of it in order to believe all of it," Jonathan said. He held eye contact with Sylvia for a moment and then she seemed to stand taller.

"And who are you, fine sir?" her father asked.

"A very dear friend of mine," Sylvia started. "I'd like you to meet Jonathan, Jonathan, this is my father Henry."

"A pleasure to meet you, sir," Jonathan said, firmly shaking the man's hand. "I know there are a lot of questions."

"I don't know where to start," Gary said, breaking his silence. "What's happened to us?" Sylvia moved to a large rock and with Jonathan's help stood atop it and looked out over the masses. Everyone stood silent and resolute, eager to hear what she had to say.

"In the dead of night, our town was attacked and everyone was kidnapped except for me. Jonathan found me and has helped in finding all of you. It's hard to explain, but you have to first understand that we *are* in another world." Gasps and whispers filed through the crowds.

"Another world?" Gary asked. "That's not possible."

"It makes perfectly logical sense," Jonathan added.

"How?"

"Worlds don't create themselves," Jonathan retorted.

"That proves nothing."

"It proves everything," Sylvia replied. "If our world back home was created by God, as we believe, then this world must also have been created by the same God. It could not have created itself, nor could anyone without the power to create such a thing, dream of doing so."

"Bottom line is we're here to take you home. All of you," Jonathan told them. "And we have a very small window to get you out of here alive." The crowd started talking excitedly. Gary held a hand up and everyone quieted down. He looked directly at Jonathan.

"We are eternally thankful to you, even if we're having a hard time showing it at this moment. Why did this happen to us? We've done nothing to these people. We don't even know who these people are. Or what this world is."

"For reasons unknown to us at the time, we were all brought to this moment for a purpose beyond what we can see. We might never know why something happened the way it did," Sylvia said.

"What's more important is how we deal with it. How we react. That shows our true character," Jonathan answered. "Perhaps the only purpose is to get our hearts focused on the right things. And get us all on the same page."

A light lit up in Gary's eyes as if he was now beginning to understand the situation.

"You seem like a fine young man," Henry said.

"And already Sylvia seems like she has grown in ways I cannot put my finger on," Gary noted. "It seems the two of you have thought of much. What do we have to do to get home?"

"Form into groups of twenty. Within a few minutes Griffins and Dreygars will begin landing. One group per animal. Climb on and you will be taken home. We already have temporary accommodations waiting until everyone is back and we will catch you all up to speed on what's happening here."

Without a moment's hesitation, Gary and Henry turned around and began calling out for the people to do as they had been told. They formed groups of twenty, and waited for the first Griffin to come into sight. The cry of a Griffin came through the sky and the people shrunk back at the sounds. Sylvia and Jonathan came forward.

"Do not fear them. They are here to help us!" Sylvia said. The Griffin landed and the first group of people hesitantly climbed aboard. Almost immediately after they took off the next one landed. Group after group followed the same pattern. Finally they climbed on themselves and were taken up into the sky. The slave camp was now completely empty and they were able to breath a sigh of relief.

"Gideon," Jonathan said into the Sactaline. "Tell Roy we've got everyone out, and we're homeward bound."

"I will, however you should know that Savannah is currently missing, Alexander seeks to go after her. Roy will be stopping briefly at Pintair while we figure out what to do."

"I don't know what to say," Jonathan said.

"It's war," Gideon replied. "But I don't think Alexander's going to take it well if he can't search for her."

185

REBELLION

"I understand."

"I'm sure you do. Get to Pintair. Send everyone else back, but wait there and join the meeting."

"Yes, sir."

*   *   *   *

Roy anxiously paced the walls of Pintair. Every Griffin had made it through without a problem and although Roy was relieved and should feel overjoyed by that fact alone, his heart was still uneasy. Alexander sat alone huddled against the wall. Roy could only imagine what he was going through, and it pained everyone to see him like this.

Cyrus had protested going back as they had expected, but had taken their counsel and gone back to the real world to be treated for his injuries. Now Geoffrey, Abby, and himself stood waiting for Jonathan to join the meeting. Jonathan came around the corner and joined their group, an awkward silence hanging over the four of them.

"We got a few surprises out of that, didn't we?" Geoffrey asked.

"More than a few," Abby replied. "At least we got all the slaves out free and clear."

"That turned out better than I had expected. I thought we'd have to fight all the way to Pintair," Roy said. "And seeing the few surprises that turned up, it seems like it was suppose to be that way."

"Savannah's still missing?" Jonathan asked. They nodded.

"Traceadox and Wiggs reported that the entire area was a cemetery. No one was left alive. At least not that they found," Roy said.

186

"How's Alexander taking it?" Jonathan asked in a whisper.

"Alexander and I are heading back to look for ourselves. Maybe we'll at the very least find her body and give him some kind of closure, but there's also the matter of Christina, who was captured."

"Should we go after her?" Geoffrey asked. "I mean I know we should, because she's your sister-in-law, but do you think it's smart? What if it's all an elaborate trap?"

"Then it's working," Roy said. "We can't just leave her; we need to rescue her. And we need to do it swiftly from what Cyrus says. Axil is not one to waste time. He will dispense with her quickly if she turns out to be worthless to him."

"He'll keep her alive for now. She won't be worth anything to him dead," Abby concluded.

Roy looked to both Jonathan and Abby. "Take care of everything in the real world. I promised Alexander one day of searching, and I'll give him one day of searching, then we'll figure out our next move."

20

"I KNOW THIS is a big risk, but thank you," Alexander said. They flew low to the ground and under the cover of the darkness, though dawn was fast approaching.

"I would be wanting to do the same thing if it was Abigail that had gone missing." Roy replied. "It was the least I could do."

"Well, again, I say thank you."

Roy nodded his head and they slowly began to descend to the battlefield near the plateaus. After a few more minutes, they spotted the first sign of a battle. Several Griffins lay dead in the forest, their riders not far from the crash site. A few minutes later they were in a sea of slain beasts and soldiers, both of the Alliance and the Kingdom.

"I hate war," Alexander said as they passed over the dead bodies.

"So do I," Roy replied. They fell silent again, both of them searching the land below. Roy studied everything intently and must have been focusing too hard or looked too serious, because Alexander smacked him in the side.

"Something wrong, Roy? You look more disturbed than I feel at the moment. What is it?"

"Everything's dead," Roy said.

"That's the story I heard, too," Alexander said, sorrow filling his voice.

"I'm not trying to make you sad, but notice the trees." Roy pointed.

"There's no leaves on them?" Alexander noted. "How's that possible? Winter's not even close to coming."

"We're landing so we can have a closer look." Alexander didn't argue as he signaled Skyquill into a controlled descent.

"Where are we exactly?"

Roy thought for a moment.

"Near the Dunland Plains. I think they're twenty-two miles north of here."

"Great. You know as well as I do the stories of the Dunland Plains."

"What tales are those?" Roy asked. Looking for a clearing to land in.

"No one ever walks in and lives to tell the tale," Alexander replied.

"The Dunland Plains are a nasty place, no arguing that, but I do think things get exaggerated just a little bit. The Dunlands are deadly, but they're not *that* deadly."

"Who says?"

"If they were that deadly, we would not '*hear*' stories." They found a clearing and landed in it. To their surprise, the warm air they had enjoyed most of their flight had turned frigid. They shivered as they pulled on their traveling cloaks over their armor.

Roy turned to Skyquill. "Keep alert and don't get too comfortable. If something goes wrong, I'll call for you." The Griffin seemed to understand and then slunk into the shadows, disappearing from the sight of anyone who might be watching.

Alexander and Roy began walking through the forest, horrified by the results of war and the carnage that lay all around. They walked for almost ten minutes in complete silence, looking into the sea of faces for any sign of Savannah. The air got cooler still and the ground became frozen and hard. Even as time went on it seemed to become heavier and harder to breath.

Finally they felt as though they couldn't go any further, their legs

189

turned to lead. They sat down on a tree stump, confused.

"What do you suppose this is?" Alexander asked, pointing to the oddities of the forest.

"Someone hiding something," Roy quickly asserted.

"I'm not completely familiar with lore concerning Dunlands. Do you think the Dunlands are near? Could that be causing it" Alexander asked.

"Dunlands have already been here!" a voice called. They turned to see a shadowy figure stepping out from behind a large tree trunk. He was dressed in a long riding coat and his wide brimmed hat, made it hard to see his eyes. His voice was deep and his speech thoughtful.

"Tracks," the man replied. "Their tracks are distinct and can be picked out a mile away if you know what you're looking for."

"And who do we have the honor of speaking to?" Alexander asked.

"Friends, my name is Gorrro," the man replied. "And who am I speaking with?"

"Captain Roy Van Doren and Alexander Reno," Roy announced.

"Please, join me by my fire and get warm."

Roy was about to ask what fire, but instead waited as the man pulled from his pocket a Sactaline of color and kind he had never seen. He set it on the ground in front of them and it burst into flames, bringing warmth and life to their souls. They looked around in astonishment as they realized even the trees had leaves on them."

"It lights, warms, and brings back to life everything its light touches," Gorrro told them. "This is a rare rock that was given to me years ago, by one who does the same thing to the soul."

"And that one is?" Roy asked. Gorrro smiled.

"At the name of Chrystar, all shall fall to their knees and proclaim his glory and honor. Even Lucerine and all the Hentar will be unable to refute him on that day!"

"So Chrystar gave you this Sactaline?" Alexander asked.

Gorrro smiled. "It has been a light in many dark places. It shows what's beneath the surface for what it really is!"

"I'm not sure I completely understand," Roy said, Alexander nodded his agreement.

"Come and see!" Gorrro stood and walked away from where they had been sitting. The Sactaline flew from its spot and hovered in the air before them, lighting up the forest. They came to a part of the forest which was littered with bodies and they understood what Gorrro had said. The light of the Sactaline touched the dead bodies of both the Kingdom soldiers and the Alliance soldiers and the difference was evident.

The bodies of the Kingdom soldiers were in perfect condition and almost seemed to have a radiance about them, as though they were only sleeping. The bodies of the Alliance soldiers were nothing but skeletal remains, as if vultures had feasted on them for a month. They retreated back to the place they had started and once again found themselves warming in front of the Sactaline.

"This is why I greeted you as 'friend'. For I could see that you are not full of vile and destructive ways."

"That is quite a gift," Roy said. Gorrro nodded.

"Why do you search for living among the dead?"

"We're looking for my wife, sir," Alexander said.

"Please, call me Gorrro. And explain your statement."

"My wife was in the battle that raged here, but last we knew she crashed. We were hoping to at least find her body, so she can rest in peace," Alexander said.

Gorrro nodded. "She rests in peace, regardless of what happens to her body, for she is now with Chrystar in the place beyond the stars."

"I know that's true, but my humanness grieves her," Alexander replied sadly.

"As you should. All would grieve if they suffered such a loss," Gorrro said. "My wife died, much the same as yours."

"I'm sorry," Roy said.

Gorrro nodded. "Three years to this day as a matter of fact." He fell quiet as if reflecting on his memories for a moment. "She was an angel, and I was anything but. However, her faith and persistence won my heart to Chrystar."

"What's your story?" Roy asked. For now, time seemed to be standing still and all both he and Alexander wanted to do was sit and talk with their new friend. Their worries were chased from the dark corners of their minds and their souls were refreshed.

"Twenty years ago the son of a bounty hunter fell in love with a beautiful young girl by the name of Erin. What is was that first attracted me I am not sure, for I did not talk to her for some time. But something about the way she talked to the other people made an impression.

"I'm from a long line of bounty hunters, some of the best there is in this part of the world. We're also the most deadly. In my day, I killed many, many people all for the chance to hand someone over and get a lot of money."

"But Erin's heart was pure and I was attracted to it, by the will of Chrystar and nothing else, her father agreed for me to marry her. I continued being a bounty hunter and did not change my ways. I treated her horribly for many many years, I was on a path to hell, destroying everything around me as I went, but still she stayed. She stood tall and proud, loving me in a way I didn't understand.

"Finally one day in a drunken rage I did what a drunken, lost, coward does to their family...I left and did not return for two full years. During those two years, my luck ran out. I never caught a single person, I burned every bridge, I destroyed myself. I see now that Chrystar let me go, and let me destroy myself because that would be the only thing that would get my attention.

"Defeated, rejected, alone, shamed, I returned to my home which I had ignored for two years. When I got within sight of the house, I cried, for there sitting on the front porch was Erin. She smiled when she saw me and made me a meal, for she could see that I had not eaten well, if at all, for some time.

"For a while I just ate, too overcome and afraid to say much of anything. She understood, somehow, and sat with me. We didn't talk, she just sat with me.

"When I was done, she asked what I wanted to do tomorrow. I was too shocked to speak, how could she not be angry with me after what I had done? She seemed genuinely happy to see me and I wasn't sure why.

"I did much apologizing and over the next few weeks we were healed from many pains. Then in the dead of night, unannounced a man arrived. The man was named Chrystar. We gave him food and drink for which he heartily thanked us. He spent the next three nights with us and then on the eve of his leaving asked what we were going to do with our lives....to further the Kingdom.

"We didn't know what to say, but somehow I think he knew that. He gave us this Sactaline and told us to put it to good use. So, we did, catching all the bad guys and helping them if we could and handing them over to other bad guys if they refused our help. My wife died three years ago when we were attacked by some associates of a person we had arrested."

"That's quite a story," Roy said, with a smile on his face. "Makes mine sound boring."

"Nonsense," Gorrro remarked. "It only sounds better in retrospect, and that's because you have the ability to look back and see Chrystar's hands moving everything behind the scenes."

"Never thought of it like that," Alexander said. They fell silent for several minutes.

"Have you found your wife among the dead?" Gorrro asked.

"No," Alexander admitted. "We're short on time and it's a very large battlefield."

"Do you suppose there are any survivors?" Roy asked.

To their surprise Gorrro nodded. "There are always survivors in a battle like this," he answered. "This battle was not waged by Dunlands. The Dunlands, if you are unfamiliar, systematically search the battlefield and kill any wounded soldiers that are not their own. However, this battle was not waged by Dunlands, it only came near their territory, which means they pillage the dead, and take survivors, if there are any."

"What for?"

"Detestable practices, sacrifices, torture, some for ransom if they are worth anything."

"Does this part of the world pay attention to what happens with the Alliance and the Kingdom."

"Of course," Gorrro replied. "The Alliance is their closest ally. Out of curiosity, what is the name of your team?"

"The A-Team," Roy replied.

A light filled Gorrro's eyes and he sat up straighter. "I have heard that name in many conversations, always with animosity and hate. If she is a part of the A-Team, they may keep her alive for torture."

"You think she's alive?!" Alexander exclaimed.

"I didn't say that. But if she is, then she would've been taken."

"Where and in what direction?" Roy asked.

"Nothing you have time for right now," Gorrro said. Their blank expressions prompted him to continue. "The Dunland do not allow any flying creature to cross their borders. They have soldiers stationed whose only purpose is to kill flying beasts. If you go in, it must be on foot, and it will take you three weeks to get there on foot."

"Three weeks," Alexander said, after being silent for a moment.

"I feel led to offer something," Gorrro said, sitting forward. "I know the ways, movements, patterns of the Dunlands. I feel as though I was put here for such a time as this." He turned to face Roy. "Captain, I offer to take Mr. Reno into the lion's den and see if we can find his wife."

Alexander's eyes widened.

"You'd do that?" Roy asked.

"In this case, I feel I'm suppose to," Gorrro said. "The will of Chrystar lays heavily on my heart. I am supposed to do this, and I will. But you will have to live with one less team member for a few weeks."

"It's a deal," Roy said shaking his hand. Alexander shook his hand too, clearly overcome with emotion. "May I have a word with Alexander privately for a moment?"

"Of course. My fire doesn't move," Gorrro said. They got up and moved away from the fire, until Roy felt they were far enough away.

"Thank you, Roy," Alexander said.

"It's the least I could do. I've heard of a Gorrro from other high clearance meetings, I have no doubt his intentions are pure. But I offer a warning."

"What is it?"

"More of a reminder. If everything with Axil goes according to how we think it will, the second door may have to be destroyed. If that happens, I don't know if we'll be able to communicate between worlds. You'll be on your own."

"I understand," Alexander said. "We will search for the third entrance."

"As will we." Roy replied.

"Maybe Gorrro will know something that we don't," Alexander said. Roy nodded.

"He knows many things, far more than he gets credit for. I too feel like we have all ended up here for this moment, though I cannot see the end."

"If we don't see each other again, it's been an honor to serve under you Roy, and you're the best friend a man could ever hope to have...obviously you're not Savannah, but you know?" They laughed.

"Yeah, I get it. Thanks for putting up with an idiot off-worlder a couple of years ago." They laughed again.

They returned to the fire and talked long into the night. When sleep overtook them they both slept peacefully and soundly. Then in the morning Roy left before they woke up. Skyquill stirred as he approached and quickly climbed to his feet.

"Just you and me now." Roy got on and Skyquill took to the sky, leaving everything behind them.

21

ROY AND SKYQUILL passed through the door at Pintair and soon landed in the crowded field in the mountains. He was greeted by many of the team, while receiving a few claps and cheers from the refugees. Already the bustling tent city had more joy than he had felt in a while. Abby quickly came to him and greeted him with a kiss.

"I'm glad you're back."

"I'm glad to be back."

"Where's Alexander?"

They slowly began walking to his tent, which he had no doubt was filled with people and they would be immediately thrust into a big meeting.

"He stayed, to search for Savannah."

"He stayed by himself?" Abby asked. By her tone Roy wasn't sure if she was pleased or worried.

"Not exactly. We met a man named Gorrro, who offered to help."

"Who?" a voice asked. They turned to see Gideon and Evelyn walking side by side. Ember, Henley and Bristol followed behind, looking at everything this new to them world had to offer. Roy smiled as he hadn't expected to see any of them.

"Gorrro," Roy answered. Gideon thought for a moment, then a light came into his eyes as if recalling a great memory.

"I know who you're talking about. He's a good soul. Now," Gideo said.

"Was he a bad soul at one time?" Abby asked.

"For a long time," Gideon replied. "Now he's a living testament to what can become of a person who surrenders his heart to Chrystar. He is hardly the same man anymore."

"So who is he?" Abby asked.

"He's quite a legend in the northern parts of the world. He can disappear in an instant, go unseen if he wishes. He deals a lot with Dunlands. The nasty bunch that they are."

"I'm not familiar with that part of the world," Abby admitted.

"You're not missing much."

"Gorrro seemed to think that if Savannah is alive, she would've been taken to one of their cities. Three weeks' walk."

"Couldn't you fly them in?" Evelyn asked

"Gorrro said it would be more dangerous to fly than walk."

"I'd believe that," Gideon remarked. "Better say your prayers. If Savannah is alive and she *is* actually a prisoner of the Dunlands, then Chrystar help her. The Dunlands are a nasty bunch, and do horrible things to their prisoners, female prisoners especially." For a moment they stood in silence.

"What did I miss while I was gone?" Roy asked.

"We'll listen to none of those questions right now. The others are anxious to have a meeting but I, as your superior officer, forbid you to show up for the next two hours. Take some time and your wife, and go relax in my own tent, because yours is filled with the things that a Captain has in his tent."

Roy and Abby smiled and began walking away.

"Roy? A word," Gideon said. Abby continued while Roy stayed back to speak with Gideon. "About that other matter, concerning the girls? They still are confused when I mentioned Cyrus's names. They don't know who he is."

Roy nodded.

"Keep them in your care for the moment, and don't tip our hand yet. When we get Christina back, we can talk about it."

Gideon and Evelyn both nodded their agreement and Roy soon joined Abby.

They prepared a quick meal and gave thanks before finding themselves down by the small stream that flowed from the mountain tops. The water was cold but refreshing as they hung their feet over the edge.

"How are you holding up with everything?" Abby asked.

Roy shrugged. "Okay, I guess."

"I don't believe you."

"I suppose it's still catching up with me," Roy admitted. "On my way here, I was thinking, it's not really the war I'm getting tired of as much as it is going between worlds. The war is just, and the Kingdom of Chrystar is one I wish to see come to fruition. But it's hard navigating two worlds at one time, when the war is now in both worlds."

"I understand." Abby said. "I've had the same struggles. My heart is sad, for although I trust Alexander is going to be okay, I know that we have a job to do. Sooner rather than later, we're probably going to have to destroy this door. If we never find the third door, we could be here forever. What then?"

"I don't know," Roy admitted.

"Ever since our cabin got blown up, I've felt like we need to be back in my world," Abby said, almost apologetically.

"Me, too," Roy said. "But I don't think this is the time for that yet."

"We have to find and destroy that third door," Abby reminded. "If we don't accomplish that, then we've wasted our time."

"I'm glad to be married to you, Abigail Van Doren."

She smiled. "That makes two of us."

REBELLION

Roy and Abby stepped into their tent. As Gideon has said, the tent was filled to the brim with people. Most of them were members of the A-Team, but others were leaders from the group stationed in Pintair. Even the various groups of refugees that they had rescued had sent representatives and offered to help in any way.

"Hello, everyone!" Roy greeted. The people all returned the greetings. "I've been out of it for a while. What's happened? We'll start with Jonathan."

"All the refugees are doing well," Jonathan told him. "We have supplies to keep them in camps for several weeks if we need to. Most of them have been finding their way back to their homes. As a precaution we have assigned one Griffin, and subsequently twenty Chrystarian Knights, to each town they return to. They've all vowed to help us in whatever way we need."

"Are we any closer to finding that third door?"

"Not yet, Roy. We're just getting back. Scouting teams were going to take to the sky tomorrow. Geoffrey also offered his assistance."

"Where is Geoffrey?"

"I'm here!" Roy heard his brother exclaim. He smiled. "Good to see you again." Roy nodded and Geoffrey knew that he had to continue with the meeting.

"Satto! How are things at Pintair?"

"It seems we pulled off the perfect heist. We were not pursued through the door and there are still no sightings of any Dreygars or Alliance soldiers within fifty miles," Satto answered.

"What about Citalia?"

"Citalia has been freed from the Alliance and stands with Chrystar."

"Glad to hear it!" Roy said. "How is Cyrus, and what is the situation with Christina?"

"Cyrus is not in good shape, but he'll live," Evelyn said. "His spirits are low, but they are raised by the fact that he still has his daughter here with him. He pleads with you to do something."

"Has any contact been made with her captor? What's his name...Axil?"

"We've delivered multiple messages to his fortress in Umble-Clar. We have not been able to make contact."

"I've been tracking his team for several days," Geoffrey said. "They're steadily heading towards Bruden."

"Do you know where they are exactly?" Roy asked.

"As close as we can know without GPS," Geoffrey said with a laugh. Roy almost chuckled too, seeing everyone else's confusion.

"He could take her to Lucerine," Jonathan said.

"He probably will. He could likely turn her in for a good sum of money. However, I don't think that's going to work as well as he thinks," Roy said.

"Why not?" Gideon asked.

"Lucerine doesn't want a traitor," Roy explained. "Maybe Lucerine would want her, to make her a display of public humiliation, as a reminder of what happens to traitors, but I don't think he's interested in that."

"If he doesn't want to make a show, than what do you think he wants then?" Geoffrey asked.

"Us."

"Us?" Geoffrey asked.

"I've heard from multiple sources that he's after off-worlders because he *thinks* they can control the doors...or something like that."

"Do you have a plan?" Gideon asked.

"Yes, I do."

"Any plan we come up with will fail," Geoffrey said. "If Axil is as smart as he seems, he knows how we think. If we come flying in-"

"Yes. He knows how we think, and I know that will make it harder to perform any kind of a rescue," Roy said. "Therefore Abigail and I have thought of a plan. It is unusual, strange, and a little on the crazy side, but we think it'll work."

"No doubt one of your off-worlder plans that will leave them guessing?" one of the others asked.

Roy nodded. "Yes."

"If we show ourselves in any way, we'll be attacked without hesitation. I know Lucerine may want the two of you, but I don't understand...what are we possibly going to do that he won't predict?" Jonathan asked.

"We're going to become bad guys."

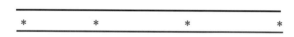

Christina slept uneasily, tied to a tree. She had fought sleep and exhaustion for as long as she had been able, but eventually she had nodded off. She had given up on trying to figure out where they were going. Her best guess was that they were headed towards Bruden.

Still, if that was the case, it did not make sense to her why Axil was insistent that they make the journey on foot. They could've easily been there in a day if they had taken a Dreygar. So for now, at least, the company of twenty-two people were traveling by foot.

It was the middle of the night and Axil was the only one with a glowing light inside his tent. The night was still and quiet and for a moment Christina imagined she could hear soft, purposely placed footsteps from the woods in front of her.

Her mind drifted to Cyrus, wishing she could speak to him again. She hung her head in defeat as she desperately wished to see their daughter Cassidy, as well. The two things she held most dear to her had been taken away.

She let her mind and heart drift for a while, but then as though a light switch had been turned on, the thoughts were chased away as her promise to Chrystar came to her memory. She would not abandon the Kingdom now. It was the only thing she had left.

Even though she may die before all of this was wrapped up, she felt peace and felt secure in her convictions. Her mind was at ease, allowing her to think of the others, as opposed to herself. She wished that her journey with the Kingdom had not ended with her being captured and taken to Bruden, but she couldn't choose that. The only thing she had to decide was how to react to what had happened.

Axil hastily strode out of the tent, holding a cup of hot liquid.

"Thirsty, Tarjinn?" He threw the liquid on her, she cried out in stunned pain. He chuckled. "Reconsider my offer and I can make this all better."

"No, thanks," Christina said.

"Fool."

"You're the fool," Christina retorted.

"Yeah, *sure.* You're the one who now has lost your husband in battle, and your daughter won't be far behind, either. You think it through and tell me if it was worth it."

Once again Christina thought she heard carefully placed footsteps. This time even Axil seemed to straighten a little. After a moment of careful listening, Axil turned to face her again.

REBELLION

"Can I get you anything, your *majesty?*" Axil mocked.

"Eat this!" a voice yelled from the side. In an instant a flash of light on steel was heard. Axil was knocked backwards, he sat up cursing and holding his head. A hooded and cloaked man jumped to the left and kicked Axil square in the chest. He toppled over and in a moment, a foot was placed on his chest. Axil cursed and then fell silent as the glowing blade of a sword was held across his throat.

"Either hold your tongue, or I'll cut it out!" the voice said. Christina's spirits surged as she recognized Roy's voice.

"Who are you?!" Axil exclaimed.

"A person you will listen to, or you will be killed!" Roy threatened. Christina watched while her mind raced. In all the times she had fought Roy or the others through the years, she felt as though she had never seen him this heated before.

"I will not-" Axil started to object. He cried out as Roy cut his forearm only slightly.

"I am not one to be trifled with!" Roy boomed. "Since you are clearly too stupid to respond to any of my team trying to contact you, I figured I'd come and pay you a visit myself."

"I have seen none of your men, and I will not bow to the whim of a liar now."

"You have no evidence to support your claim, and I *can* prove that. My people have been in contact with you ten times over the past two days, five of those requests coming in person. We've been tracking you from the air, so you're location is not a surprise or a mystery to us."

"What is your point in this?" Axil exclaimed.

To Christina's surprise, Roy let Axil get up and then two other team members rushed in and held him from behind. They easily removed his weapons. It was only now that both she and Axil realized that everybody else in the camp was sitting tied up outside of their tents.

204

When had that happened?

"Tarjinn is useless to you. A traitor is a traitor, yes, but she's not the prize that Lucerine wants," Roy said.

"I need to bring him something so I myself am not the one on the chopping block," Axil responded.

"Explains why you're walking," Roy said. "You're trying to buy yourself time."

"I can fabricate any story I need to, in order to keep myself alive."

"So you admit that she's useless to you?"

Axil directed a hard and icy glare at her.

"Yes," Axil admitted. "She's useless, but I still have a job to do."

"Then why not do it with something that is sure to please your master?" Roy said. A sly smile spread across his face.

"What did you have in mind?"

"A trade between enemies, that will benefit both of us. Myself and my brother Geoffrey for Tarjinn."

"You wouldn't actually-"

"If I wouldn't then why am I here?" Roy asked. The conviction in Roy's voice clearly startled Axil.

"When?"

"Three days from now. At the Harforl Bridge. Do you know where that is?"

"Near the ruins of Pintair, I think. I've never been there before."

"Perhaps you should look at a map," Roy said, casually pulling one from his pocket and dropping it at Axil's feet.

"What if I say no?"

"Then I have a squadron of two hundred Griffins ready to lay waste to your precious *Umble-Clar.*"

"And I suppose you'll kill me if I don't agree?"

"Heck, no. We'd leave you alive. Watch you crawl back to Lucerine and see what happens to you."

"You're sick," Axil said. Christina had to stifle a laugh.

"Yes, but do we have an agreement?" Roy asked.

Axil stared at Roy and then at Christina.

"Yes. I'll give you the wench for you and your brother. But no surprises!"

"Of course not. We'll be there," Roy said, beginning to back away. The other two people released Axil, who was still without his weapons. "A word of warning. I will be keeping my squadron of two hundred Griffins near your fortress. You'll have a squadron of twenty watching your progress from the sky. If you falter from your course or if you lay a hand on Tarjinn, we will destroy Umble-Clar, exactly like I said."

In that moment, Axil looked more defeated and angry than Christina had ever seen him before.

Roy and the rest of his team withdrew further. "Better untie your men and get started. It's a long journey on foot." Griffins called through the air. Roy turned to walk away and met eyes with Christina. He gave her a wink and then left.

22

CHRISTINA TRIED TO calm her own nerves as the next three days went by. Despite the fact that she had a strong leading that everything would work out, she wasn't exactly sure how that would happen. The uncertainty gnawed at her, and Axil wasn't getting any more agreeable as they approached the ruins of Pintair.

He was certainly making a good effort to double cross Roy and the A-Team, but she doubted any of it would actually work. He had sent out a number of the people from the group with messages calling for aid and support. Some of the people never returned, but eventually one of them did and brought with him word of several thousand Dreygars being sent to help capture the two off-worlders.

For now, Christina was in the dark about what was actually going to happen. She was tied to the back of a cart, having been forced to walk now that her injuries were healed enough that she could do so. True to his word though, no hand was laid on Christina during their travels to Pintair. Perhaps another sign that Axil was still uncertain about what would happen.

Slowly the forest around them began to give way as they came to what Christina knew was the ruins of Tunlet. It was really a part of Pintair, but far enough apart to be its own small city. She knew little history of the place other than she and her sisters used to play here as kids. Much like they did in the Ruins of Pintair.

"Stop here!" Axil yelled out. The company, which had dwindled down to only ten people stopped and threw down their packs and bags. "Untie the wench. We go on alone."

One of the men came and untied Christina while Axil talked in hasty, hushed tones to one of the other men who vanished into the trees. Christina was swiftly fitted with a rope around her neck as though she was cattle and brought to him.

"Well, here we are. We started this journey together, it's only fitting that we end it together I suppose," Axil said. "It's a shame, though. You were one of the best."

"By whose standards?" Christina asked. Axil scoffed.

"Do you really think that your new friends will succeed in this trade? When I'm done, I will have two off-worlders to hand over to Lucerine, who will be arriving in a little while."

"Congratulations," Christina mocked. Axil pulled his hand back but didn't strike her even though he clearly wanted to.

"I have decided that Roy is right about one thing. You are useless to me as a trade. But I have other things in mind, starting with taking you to my private wing of my fortress at Umble-Clar."

"You'll die there then?" Christina threatened.

"I'm quite certain weapons will be nowhere to be found." Axil chuckled.

"That's because, if it came down to a duel you know who would win."

"How little you know," Axil replied. "Without weapons, what could you possibly do to me?"

"I don't need weapons," Christina said. Axil's confidence seemed to shift, ever so slightly.

"I'll make sure there are plenty of soldiers to put you into submission, should you need it."

"Am I flinching?" Christina said, drilling Axil with a look that clearly rattled him.

He didn't speak to her any further, instead calling one of the other people to him and uttering something in a language she didn't understand. They waited where they were for nearly a half hour until one of Axil's men, cloaked and hooded, came running into the camp.

"Van Doren is here!" the messenger said.

"Which one?"

"There are only two men, one is Roy. I can only assume the second is his brother."

"Any other sightings of Roy's team?"

"We eliminated nearly fifty people this morning. He's got no friends here," the messenger said. Axil let out a sadistic chuckle.

"Then, by all means, let's get this party started!" Axil exclaimed to his group. They all shared his excitement. "The wench and I will go and make the trade. Be ready for victory!"

She was yanked along by the rope around her neck at a pace that proved that Axil knew he had the upper hand. Axil happily yanked her through the woods and the shattered buildings until finally reaching the Harforl Bridge. It spanned a great gap of nearly one hundred yards and was wide enough to easily accommodate a host of soldiers crossing at once. Far below a river flowed into the sea.

On the opposing side of the bridge, she could see Roy and Geoffrey without weapons, waiting as they had said they would. Christina's pulse quickened as Axil shoved her in front of him and touched the blade of a crudely shaped knife to her back.

"No surprises now, sweetheart," Axil whispered. Next he spoke loudly to Roy. "Here I am! True to my word!"

"I'm surprised," Roy replied.

"I figured you would be!" Axil yelled, sounding a little too excited.

"Actually, I was surprised you didn't figure it out sooner."

"Or at all," Geoffrey added. Axil hesitated. Christina allowed herself to smile.

"Well, Van Doren's, thank you for surrendering so peacefully. You've made this very easy."

"You're welcome," Roy replied. The response clearly rattled Axil. "Thank you for not looking to closely."

"What are you talking about?"

Roy whistled and the messenger that had talked to them appeared from behind them. "You really should think about some other disguise rather than a black cloak with a hood." The messenger pulled his hood off, revealing it to be one of Roy's Team members, though which one it was Christina couldn't remember. "It does make infiltrating rather easy."

To Christina's surprise, the rest of Axils people came forward and lowered their hoods, revealing them to also be part of The A-Team.

"Oh, and I'm sorry, but I don't think your Alliance friends could make it," Geoffrey said. He motioned and the messengers that had been sent out over the past couple of days were produced, effectively tied and gagged.

"You'll never get away with this!" Axil screamed.

"You're probably right," Roy said. He looked to Geoffrey as if looking for a second opinion. Geoffrey seemed to be mulling over something.

"Maybe I'm wrong, Roy, but didn't we just get away with this?"

Roy nodded. "He's got a good point!"

Axil was speechless for a moment. "You'll never get away! Kill me and your chances are better. Otherwise, I'll just go get help and hunt you to the ends of the earth."

"What do you think?" Roy asked Geoffrey.

"I think it sounds like a pretty good threat."

"I'll give it that." Roy turned to Axil again. "We were already figuring on that."

"Let me be perfectly clear!" Axil exclaimed. "You won't be getting Tarjinn alive if you're going to do this to me." He twisted the knife ever so slightly. Christina grimaced in pain.

"He knows how to bargain," Geoffrey said.

"Yeah, it's too bad he doesn't know about that other thing."

"What other thing?" Axil asked.

"I think it speaks for itself," Roy said. "Though I would suggest getting out of the way so you don't get run over by a crazy lady!"

Christina and Axil both whirled around in fear as they heard the strangest, most frightening sound either of them had ever heard before. It started out as a loud rumble and steadily grew as something raced towards them.

A woman's cry of exhilaration came above the noise and in a moment an old pickup truck came bounding through the forest. It hit a slight incline flying for several feet before landing on the bricks of the city. The truck screeched noisily as the truck was sent into a tail spin.

Christina quickly moved out of the way, while Axil frantically jumped and tripped to the ground. The truck came to a stop. Abby was in the front seat, with the largest smile on her face that she could've imagined.

"Get in, girl! We've gotta go!" Abby yelled.

Christina didn't hesitate as she did what she was told. Every other member of Roy's team, including Roy and Geoffrey, jumped into the back of the truck, firing a number of arrows at the bridge as they left it behind them. Christina held on for dear life as Abby sent the truck rocketing through the old streets and alleys of Pintair.

Finally, after the scariest ride any of them had ever been on, Abby brought the truck to a screeching halt just short of the door that would take them back to the other world. Roy slowly came out of the back of the truck and grabbed on to Abby's door, fear and shock on his own face. Abby smiled innocently at him.

"I love this truck! I love it!" Abby shouted. They all laughed.

"That was terrifying," Roy said. "Christina, are you alright?"

"My sister-in-law is a crazy lady," she replied.

"You'll get used to it," Roy said. Screeches came through the sky and within two minutes, the entire two hundred Griffins that had been stationed near Umble-Clar had passed through the door and vanished from the world they were in. Roy looked at Abby, who gave him a look he knew all to well.

"You're not going to get out of the truck are you?"

"Heck, no! I'm having fun."

"Just remember the cave is much smaller than the great outdoors."

"I know! It's going to seem like we're going so much faster!" Abby exclaimed. Roy was speechless.

"Just get us back alive, hon," Roy said, before climbing in the back again.

Abby looked at Christina a funny glint in her eye. "Are you ready?"

"I know Cyrus is on the other side, so Lord willing, we'll live to tell about this tale."

"You'll think of it and laugh later on." Without hesitation Abby pressed the accelerator all the way to the floor. The tires screeched noisily as it was launched towards the cliff. They hit the door and were in the dark cave.

"Now for the fun part!" Abby yelled.

"What do you mean?" Christina asked. Her question was pointless as explosions rang out behind them. Roy and the others were shooting arrows at the cave, collapsing the door so it could never be used again. Christina's heart pounded as Abby rocketed through the cave and the flames seemingly got closer and closer to them, all the while Abby screamed like a little girl who had just gotten a birthday present.

Finally, light appeared ahead of them and to everyone's surprise, Abby slowed the truck to a gentle roll as they exited the cave. Roy and his team shot a few final arrows into the cave, collapsing it completely. The greeting they received was almost more than Christina could take. Every person who had been aboard a Griffin was making a tremendous sound as they cheered for their leaders who had returned. Christina looked around, seeing not only warriors from her world but also a slew of tents arranged everywhere you might imagine.

"Are those . . .?"

"Yes," Abby said. "Those are all the slaves. We got them all out!" The next few minutes were a blur as everyone celebrated and then was gently sent back to their duties by Roy and Abby.

The three of them climbed in and Abby drove them to the middle of the ever-growing camp where their very big tent was set up. They climbed out of the truck and Christina followed behind the two of them as they entered into a sight that took her breath away.

Cyrus sat upright in a bed, bandages all over, but a smile was on his face. Sitting on his lap was their daughter Cassidy, happily giggling at the stupid face Cyrus was making. Their nanny, Rosett, sat alongside. All of them looked happier than she had seen them in a long time. Including herself. Cyrus smiled when he saw her.

"As happy as this moment is, I think it needs one more thing," Abby said. She motioned around the corner, Gideon and Evelyn walked in, Ember, Henley and Bristol in tow. They excitedly ran and embraced Christina who was speechless, wondering if this was a dream. She looked back at Roy and Abby who were smiling as much as she was.

"Go," Abby told her. "There will be time for meetings, planning, and work later. Enjoy your family. We'll see you tonight." Christina watched as the two of them, hand in hand, turned and headed out of the tent.

REBELLION

"Well, Mr. Van Doren, I think that went pretty well!" Abby praised.

Roy smiled. "I love it when a plan comes together."

"There's that line again."

"Hey, we're the A-Team, I have to use it every now and then."

"I'm still not sure what this whole A-Team thing is in your world," Gideon called out as they walked up to them.

"Looks like we'll be here for a while, so maybe we'll get to find out," Evelyn said.

"A little harder, seeing your cabin is a pile of rubble," Geoffrey said as he joined the group.

"There's always the internet or cable," Roy suggested, to which he got the reaction he had wanted. Confusion.

"How is a net supposed to help?" Evelyn asked.

Roy and Geoffrey chuckled. "Never mind."

"I know you're going to ask, and I tried the moment you came out of the cave," Gideon started. "We can't contact the other world. Until we find that third door, we are on our own."

"So we can't contact Alexander and Gorrro?" Abby asked.

"That's right."

"How are Jonathan and Sylvia doing?"

"Very well. The airport has been fully renovated to handle any number of Griffins or Dreygars we might throw at it," Gideon answered. "And the *'Berry High Flier'* will soon be joining the search."

"I still can't believe you named your plane that," Roy remarked.

"You're just jealous," Geoffrey said. "What's your Griffin's name?

Skywalker, or something like that?"

"Skyquill! Get it right," Roy replied. "Trust me, I suggested Skywalker and that was thoroughly rejected."

"By who?"

"By him."

"The animal decides his name?"

"Yes, partly."

"That's absurd!"

"No, what's absurd is when we were kids, you named *our* cat 'dog.'"

"And the problem is?"

"The poor animal has no idea what he was!" Roy exclaimed. "Just like that dog whose name was Midnight!"

"Was he a black dog?" Abby asked. Roy nodded. "Seems fair."

"But Geoffrey over here, called him 'Pig' so whenever he wanted to call the dog he stepped out the door and yelled *'Here, pig!'* and the dog came running."

"I think I will forbid you both from naming animals ever again," Abby teased. They all laughed and walked through the tent.

"So tomorrow we'll start our work?" Geoffrey asked.

"That's right. We have a lot of work to do and not much time to do it."

"What do you think the Alliance will do when they learn about what happened?" Geoffrey asked.

"They'll come back fighting, no doubt," Roy answered. "But Chrystar has a plan."

"Do you know what the plan is?" Abby asked. Roy and Gideon exchanged a humorous glance.

"I might," Roy said.

"And you haven't told me?!" Abby exclaimed.

"I could tell you, but then I'd have to kill you," Roy said. Everyone else laughed as they watched the three of them walk away bantering back

REBELLION

and forth with each other.

23

SAVANNAH STRUGGLED TO open her eyes. She lay on a large slab of black stone. She reached for her head and jerked her hand away when she felt dried blood matted in her hair. Carefully she pushed herself off the ground and took in the world around her.

She shivered in the cold and she could now see that the slab of rock that she was on seemed to be floating in air. Carefully, she moved to the edge and looked down onto the city that was indeed below her.

At least a thousand feet separated her and the highest building, which was made out of a rough red rock of some kind. Torches and Sactalines lit up the city and the moon and the stars could not be seen.

In the air above the city she could see hundreds of rock slabs, like she was on, floating in the air. Confused and frightened, her thoughts turned to Alexander and everyone else she loved.

Where were they? Were they dead? Did they think she was dead? A thousand questions peppered her soul, but at the same time a peace came over her and she began to focus on the only thing she could do.

Try to escape.

She studied the rock and surroundings, wondering what she could possibly use to escape. She looked down, noticing for the first time that her armor and normal clothes were gone and she was wrapped in a tattered grey robe.

217

REBELLION

In an instant, the slab of rock slowly began moving through the sky, taking her somewhere else in the city. She studied everything as she began flying by other rock slabs. People were on each one, everyone stuck in their own individual prison.

A while later, a large black building jutted up out of the barren landscape. A single rectangular opening glowed yellow on the edges. Savannah took a deep breath and said a prayer as the platform picked up speed, heading for the opening.

To Be Continued...